CRIPPLED

KINGS

MARQUIS BOONE

MARQUIS BOONE
enterprises

CRIPPLED KINGS

MBE books may be ordered through booksellers or by visiting www.marquisboone.com

Because of the nature of the Internet, any web address or links contained in this book may have changed since publication and may no longer be valid. The views expressed in this work are solely those of the author and do not necessarily reflect the views of the publisher, and the publisher herby disclaims any responsibility for them.

ISBN: 978-0-9887873-7-7 (paperback)
ISBN: 978-0-9887873-8-4 (ebook)

Printed in the United States of America

MBE Publishing rev. date: 06/15/2014

Other Books by Marquis Boone
Available Wherever Books Are Sold

 Closer To Your Dream

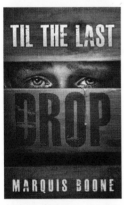 'Til The Last Drop

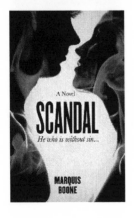 Scandal

DEDICATION

This story is dedicated to every man that walks this earth. This book is dedicated to the king in you and to the women and children that are connected to them. It is dedicated to those who rule with a limp and to those who feel impeached, forsaken, rejected, and unworthy. May this book bring clarity, freedom and healing.

CONTENTS

The stories you are about to read are true and based on actual events documented and found in Dr. Royal's case files.

NONDISCLOSURE

"**O**ver the years I've been trusted with others secrets." Michael Royal leaned against the wall inches from the floor to ceiling diamond-sharp plate glass window. Rays of the sun reflected from the lake behind the office building of his compound. Royal turned and smiled at Gabriel "Someone has to help the men who help everyone."

Gabriel nodded as he stared at Royal. His head dropped into his hands. The brevity of his mentors confessions over the last few times they met settled around his shoulders. Broad and strong, he hoped they could hold the new weight being prepared for them.

Royal lowered himself into the chair in front of Gabriel. "Nondisclosure is the most valuable asset of the Royal Treatment Center and the currency is trust. Not one person is to ever know the services our clients receive unless our client tells them; which includes secretaries, spouses, children and parents. We are responsible for providing an elite level of security to the most powerful men in the world. That is why we prefer English-speaking clients...translators weaken the ability to keep what we do here private."

"We never make concession? Men ruling in Africa, the Middle East and other places plagued with violence may need your services."

Gabriel's brow furrowed. Anxiety and frustration attempted to sidle up his spine.

Royal threw his head back and laughed. He shook his head. "Men from foreign soil able to afford services here have learned English from the time they learned to speak - in addition to Spanish, and a native tongue. These are the men who determine the degree the world tilts on its axis. Not one person has been revealed as a client by anyone who works here now and we've only had one person to leave. Our employees are more than satisfied, which is why we have a zero attrition rate. The four to six month hiring process seems daunting and over the top. But our lowest paid janitorial staff member makes more than the average entry level CEO. No one has any reason to ever betray the trust instilled in them by the Royal family so they never have a reason to betray the trust given to us by our clients. If nothing else, over these next few weeks, I'm going to need you to take that with you. Trust, Gabriel, is everything."

"Are you sure about this?" Gabriel looked around the office. He settled back into the buttercream lambskin pillows with a sigh. Thirty-two karat gold trimmed the accents on the desk, the frame holding a life size portrait of the founder of The Royal Treatment Center, David Royal. His shoes sunk into the carpet as if it were created from memory foam. His mind wandered to the first time his father brought him to the facility. "These men are treated like gods. I'm just one man and what if they find out about me?"

"What if they don't?" Royal leaned forward and tapped Gabriel's knee.

Gabriel's eyes flew open.

"This is the only place some of them are able to relax and some of them, despite the ridiculous amount of money they spend to be here, are still unable to do so and deal with what drove them here. They may be treated like gods, but you and I both know they are far from divine. Every man who comes here is broken, irretrievably and in some cases shattered but all of them who walk through those gates are crippled in some way."

Gabriel sighed. "The Yates family created a foundation in his memory. His remains haven't been found, but they treat his disappearance as a death and I'm responsible. He followed my suggestion."

Royal closed his eyes, "You're the best in the business at what you do, Gabriel. And we all have those cases where despite all of our best and sometimes overreaching measures, the men see themselves as beyond repair and live that truth. My case load over the years has ended with more clients restored than failures, but the clients who weren't happy haunted me. A few still haunt me. I'm going to have some serious explaining to do when I meet my maker. Listen, when we meet over these next few weeks and I'll finish this training knowing I helped you do this better than I did."

Gabriel chuckled. "That is impossible, you are the best."

Sadness and regret covered Royal's face for a moment. He held contact with Gabriel. "You consider the Yates case a great tragedy, and it is, but not because you failed him, he failed himself. I've had several cases that left me questioning the existence of a need for this company. Seems like I've been attempting to help the client I've failed the most."

Gabriel straightened his spine as a chill ran through his body. The temperature in the room seemed to drop several degrees.

Royal shifted in his seat to look out at the lake. "The most important part of helping the clients, outside of the need for trust, is the desire of the person to be restored. Some of these men have been taught how to cope without being taught how to work through what caused the need for them to see us. No matter how much money, fame, admiration, sex and power a man has, if he is unable to be honest with himself about who he is, where he came from and love who he's become ...no matter how the world sees him, he'll always be a crippled King. That is the case for my hardest client. I can't tell you his name because he's still in treatment, but he is a hard one. That might be why after all these years, some days it feels as if he hasn't made any progress despite all the work he's put in to move beyond his disability."

"You keep seeing him even though he doesn't think he is making progress?" Gabriel said.

"Some days he seems that way and others feel as though he is about to take things to the next level. Just depends on the day-which is what frustrates me. All of the people I've helped have some malicious reasons they have become crippled. For this client despite the tragedy of it all, his disability is something he couldn't control... an accident. And all that is required of him is to accept what happened, train to become what he can be today and move on." Royal laughed. "I sound like an announcer on an infomercial."

Gabriel chuckled. "How can an accident interfere with a man's ability to succeed if he's been talking to you for more than a day?I've seen winos decide to become sober after five minutes with you."

"Foolish things confound the wise, Gabriel. No one suspects your weakness. You try everyday to live as though it never happened, yet you're ashamed of it and it has an explicable root."

"Sorry, sir." Gabriel dropped his head.

"Nothing to apologize for. I'm not talking about you. The client I am talking about was the innocent bystander of a family feud. The client was struck down by a family member after they argued with his parents and suffered because they didn't see him. Now the average person isn't able to see it, but this client hasn't been able to forgive the person he holds responsible for losing what he considered everything and that has tortured him all of his life." Michael nodded, "We don't treat many clients with unstable results, but sometimes you meet one or two who you almost can't let them go...you will learn how to see who, if left alone, would create a life detrimental to the reputation and success they enjoyed before they became clients. Understand?"

Gabriel relived walking through the halls as an intern twenty-five years earlier. He never imagined a place where 32 karat gold was used as paint on accents. The titanium, platinum and ivory trim strong enough to hold the weight of ten men lined the walls of the entire complex. Every ceiling in every room, including the spa, workout center and bathrooms were outfitted with the cutting edge trims, track lighting and industrial strength lifts because David Royal didn't want anyone able to afford the services to feel they weren't able to access the facilities. Despite being in an undisclosed-to-most area with pentagon level security measures, Gabriel still recognized the beauty and serenity resting at The Royal Treatment Center and wanted to make sure it lived on no matter what. "Yes, Sir, I understand."

GENESIS CASES

Gabriel entered Royal's office with a sigh. The new client and extra cases transitioned from the birth of a junior counselor's newborn child exhilarated and exhausted him. He'd seen Royal juggle what appeared to be three times as many cases so he refused to complain.

Royal dropped down onto the sofa and motioned for Gabriel to sit in the counselor's chair.

Gabriel paused, "Really? In your seat?"

Royal's rich baritone filled the crisp air. "It's imperative you glean as much from me as possible from this moment on. I'm still trying to help my client we talked about last time, but I want to walk you through what I call my genesis cases."

"Genesis cases?" Gabriel cleared his throat. He sat back in the chair trying to settle into the imprint made by his mentor.

"The answers to the problems for many of my clients are based on the things I took away from eight cases." Royal lay back on the sofa and closed his eyes. "A few clients still come in three or four times a year or during times of stress, and some didn't recover at all; but all of them formed the foundation for the Royal Treatment approach which, as you know, has worked well for our clients and employees."

Gabriel nodded. He cut his counseling teeth using the Royal Treatment techniques with great success, for most of his clients. Nothing would stop him from learning Royal's secrets so his success rate would be as close to perfect as possible going forward.

"You get my message from Ms. Barnes to bring your iPad? I asked her to message you before you came." Royal looked around Gabriel's feet.

Tap. Tap. After several seconds passed the door slid open with no sound. A brown skinned woman with silver streaks throughout her shoulder length locks entered. An apologetic smile was aimed toward the men as they turned to face the door. She took quick steps toward them holding a leather case. "Mr. Jonas, your assistant, apologized for not getting this to you before you left for your time with Royal."

Gabriel placed his hand over hers and kissed it as he accepted his tablet. "Thank you, Ms. Barnes. I'm gonna have her train with you again. Though if cloning were legal, we wouldn't have this problem."

Ms. Barnes blushed. Her hand waved in Gabriel's direction. "Hush, perfection is an illusion. Give her time; she'll do better, and with all the cases you just received, I'm surprised she didn't forget her own head. Be merciful, Gabe; it will win you more allies than anything else you give your co-workers. She may work for you, but she'll be more invested in your success when you work with her."

Gabriel turned to Royal.

Royal nodded, "She taught me everything I know."

Ms. Barnes shook her head with a chuckle. "I'll bring lunch in about ninety minutes, gentlemen."

"Ms. Barnes? Hard to believe she is your secret weapon." Gabriel shook his head and turned back toward Royal.

"Believe it. I don't know if the Royal Treatment Center would even be here after my Dad died if it weren't for Ms. Barnes. She is the reason Oscar Tyler received 'Father of the Year' last year from his hometown. He was on the brink of bankruptcy when he came."

"Oscar Tyler , coach of the Chicago Cubs and Hall of Famer?" Gabriel's mouth hung open for a moment. He opened a new file on his iPad. "I'm listening."

"Like I said, Ms. Barnes is the reason he has a relationship with his children and is alive to enjoy it. He made money being the man but had no idea what being a father meant, and a good reason for not knowing...he'd never known one as a child."

***

"You can't date her, boy! That is your cousin. First cousin, because I'm your father. So put it back in your pants and go back over the fence." Mr. Young cleared his throat and spit on the ground to the left of Oscar's feet.

The world stopped spinning as the words made Oscar's head spin. His father's hands slid under each arm as his legs gave out for a second. "Dad?"

Mr. Thomas shook him until he straightened up. "That's Mr. Thomas, to you. You're not to breathe a word of this to anyone. My wife and family live here and that is why any little girl you see come around here is off limits to you."

His green eyes flashed with anger, disbelief and pain as he stared into Royal's eyes. "What kind of bastard does that to a child? He lived next door to me for five years with no more than a wave, then dropped that shit on me as if he was telling me my shoestring was untied. The ironic thing about it is that I idolized him before that moment. He moved back into the house after his mother died and became the director of the community center, breathing life into the neighborhood. I learned how to play baseball on his team. That is my memory."

Royal wrote on his pad, "So that is your most painful memory?...I asked you for your favorite memory and most painful memory."

"And I gave you both. My mother refused to acknowledge I existed. She never came for any holidays and barely sent money to pay my aunt for taking care of me. For one moment, I had a parent I could see. He gave me something I never expected to have - a mirror and the tiniest bit of hope." Oscar let a low, hard pained laugh escape his throat. "Until it hurt more to hope than recognize the truth."

Royal leaned forward. "What was that?"

"I am nobody's somebody." Oscar shook his head, "I felt lower than the spit I stepped over to climb the fence back to my Aunt Glenda's house. You know the entire time I lived with her she never told me, I love you, never said, I'm proud of you, never spoke a positive word to me. Not even when I was signed to play for the league. Third highest signed player in MLB history and not one nice word. But her hand was out in front of everyone else's and after everyone else's was gone."

Royal wrote something else down on the pad. "She had to love you to let you move back in two years ago. As a grown man with twelve children and no job."

Oscar's stare was hard enough to pierce titanium. He swung his long legs over the side of the couch. "Strangers take stray dogs home. After all the money I gave her and those raggedy people at her church, the least she could do was let me move back into the house I paid off for her twice."

"Twice? How..." Royal shook his head. "She loved you the best she could, just like your mother. Imagine the other options your mother had as a married woman pregnant with a child from an extra-marital affair. Abortion? Adoption? Dumpster? How is your relationship now?"

"I told you I'm nobody's somebody. She walked away from me before I turned one year old and never looked back. The only time they talked about me was to arrange finances and some years, based on how that asshole she married felt, she didn't do that. He's still alive; so to her I'm still dead." Oscar laughed again. "No amount of money I spent was enough for her to acknowledge me in public, but I know she was one of those invisible church projects my aunt solicited help for when that no good husband of hers didn't feel like working."

"So your parents weren't able to love you the way you needed. You're justified in how you are making sure not to do the same thing to your kids." Royal leaned back in his chair. "Acknowledging your children makes you a better parent to them than your parents were to you. But if that is your only goal, you are not much better than them. Your kids deserve to be *your* somebodies.

Oscar's eyes turned amber red with anger. "My children know I love them."

"Your children know you made them." Royal wrote something down on the paper. "Your child support is as inconsistent as your mother's to your aunt at times, especially for the younger children. Tell me how you have learned from your pain and confronted your fear of rejection and being abandoned to be there for them the way they need you?"

Tap. Tap. Tap. Ms. Barnes peeked her head into the door. "Mid-session break. It's lunch time and I have Oscar's favorite, like I promised last time he came."

The flame in Oscar's eyes dampened and tears replaced it. "You...you remembered something I told you two months ago."

Ms. Barnes wheeled the sterling silver plate settings on the matching service cart into the room. A smile lit her face and the room up as she placed Oscar's lunch in front of him.

Royal rubbed his hands together as she placed his lunch on the table to the left of his chair. He motioned for her to sit next to Oscar while his client's head was bent in prayer.

"I knew there was something undeniable about you, you have a great deal of faith." Ms. Barnes looked into Oscar's eyes.

He shook his head. "God only hears from me when I'm hungry and in trouble, not much faith required for that, ma'am."

She gave a gentle shove to the knee closest to her. "Nonsense. Some folks don't have the sense to thank Him for providing a meal or to call Him when they need Him. Give yourself credit for knowing that if no one else came to your aid, God always has and always will. Hope I'm not out of place, Mr. Royal. You see I know we all need counseling and what we do here is necessary and I have seen the miracles that happen, just like it will for you, if you want...but never discount how strong your faith has to be to acknowledge you rely on Him for provision and help. He is a good Father and the best Dad. That is why He even gives it to the ones who don't know to ask."

A look passed over Oscar's face as Ms. Barnes stood from the couch. "Yes ma'am."

"I'll send someone to retrieve those plates when you buzz again, Mr. Royal. I apologize again for stepping out of line. You know how I can get. See you later, Mr. Tyler." Ms. Barnes made a quiet exit as the weight of her words settled into Oscar's soul with each bite of his food.

"I can't," Oscar sat his plate on the coffee table next to the crystal glass filled with aqua-infused water.

Royal looked up from his plate. "You can't what?"

"I can't tell you how I give my children what they need. I don't know how to give them more than what I've given them...that is why I'm here." Oscar looked at the door. "She for real?"

Royal smiled. "She is the real deal. If she said it, she saw it in you and she meant it. I have clients who've never heard her say more than 'Mr. Royal will see you now.' She broke protocol to speak into you; that almost never happens."

Oscar smiled. "That right?"

"That's right." Royal dabbed the napkin to the corners of his mouth. He wrote something on his notepad. "So after that day, when did you speak with your father again?"

Sadness filled Oscar's features. "Who said we ever spoke again? I haven't spoken to him since he told me about my first cousin. Guess he didn't have anything else to say."

Royal nodded. "You believe what Ms. Barnes said about you?"

Oscar rolled his eyes and shook his head.

"You remember the feeling that spread through you when you found out about your oldest child?" Royal leaned toward Oscar.

"Excitement, fear and dread." Oscar's chin touched his chest as his head dropped.

Confusion crossed Royal's face. "Take me back to that moment."

***

Gabriel sat his iPad on the table to the left of Royal's chair. He strolled over to the window and looked at the lake behind the office buildings. "He didn't think he was worth a few kind words? Six of the MLB records he broke have never been touched or even attempted to be matched since he retired. So his parents were horny teens and his aunt came from the generation that said, I love you, with a roof, clothes on your back, shoes on your feet and a roof over your head. What did Ms. Barnes do for him?"

"No one had ever broken the rules to show they cared for him that couldn't get something in exchange for being kind to him. You've read the treatment agreement, our staff is here to serve not to counsel," Her words could have cost her job. Anything more than work-related communication could cost her more than he believed he was worth. One meal and a few kind words were enough for him to agree to come back to the next session."

Royal cleared his throat. "You don't see the root of Oscar's problems?"

Gabriel shrugged. "Things outside of your control shouldn't be able to control who you become and what you do with your life. His parents and aunt weren't the best, but they didn't beat him or molest him. How is what he endured enough to make his case one to learn how to help other people? Most people have one person in childhood who showed them love. Oscar had to have one person who loved him for more than what he could do for them."

"You are thinking like a counselor, from the perspective of someone loved by at least one person. Twelve children with a father whose ideal of being a good Dad was acknowledging them meant twelve people born into this world would be forced to deal with the same abandonment and rejection issues that left Oscar with an emotional handicap. He couldn't recognize something he'd never seen... that's like asking a victim to identify an attacker who assaulted them from behind."

"Twelve children-someone loved him, Royal." Gabriel returned to the seat.

"Yes, several people loved him, which is why he is still here today, but he didn't know how to recognize or receive love by the time he encountered people who wanted to give it to him. As an athlete and champion, he was a king; but in his private life he didn't function. Dysfunction is why he came to us."

"Every man is born with the potential to be a king in their own right, Gabriel. But somewhere through the growth process men incur mental, physical, emotional and even spiritual injuries that truly leave them cripple. That's why they come here - because a small percent understand that they don't have to continue to help others and heal others while they are wounded." Royal looked at his mentee as if he could will all the things he'd seen over the years into the younger counselor's psyche. "Oscar found peace with his past, which is why now he has a beautiful family. He married one of the most loving women I've ever met, but he broke lots of hearts on the way to her and turned away some stellar women because he didn't know how to accept the love they wanted to give him."

"I can't imagine turning away genuine love from a beautiful woman. No man with the good sense God gave him can turn away a good woman." Gabriel said.

"How a man responds to the love of a great woman says a lot about who he is when she offers her love. Who we choose is part of our spiritual journey. A man with a mature emotional intelligence will choose a great woman who will help him elevate to a higher level. A great woman inspires a man. When a man rejects a great woman or chooses a lesser woman, he doesn't want to or know how to do what is necessary to be the king that great woman sees within him. The character or lack of development of a man is reflected in the woman he receives and loves." Royal leaned back and closed his eyes.

"So Ms. Barnes words helped him become able to be a greater man with one encounter after years of breaking the hearts of some of the finest women on Earth and fathering children with them. I'm missing something." Gabriel scoffed.

"So was Oscar, but he found it; and his wife of the last eight years and their happy children is the proof he did. He did have me worried for a while after the first session we had about co-parenting and romantic relationships." Royal laughed. "He had us all concerned."

***

"You know her crazy ass showed up at the stadium. I just landed this position... on a probationary period." Oscar paced back and forth in front of Royal's chair. "I almost had to physically restrain her. Seven months pregnant in high heels and trying to fight some chick I work with I'm not even doin."

"This is the first time Shaqwanaya embarrassed you this way?" Royal's pen hovered over the pad. The logo for the center embossed above the fine lined sheet of paper.

Oscar stopped in his tracks. His head dropped. "I'm not proud of what I've done, and I reached out to all of them, every last one of them to tell them I'm getting help and want to be in my kids lives. Shaqwanaya showed up at Tatayana's baby shower livid when she started showing two months ago, but I had security looking for her so they didn't get to see each other."

"You have both women pregnant at the same time. You don't see why she'd be upset about that?" Royal said.

Oscar walked around the coffee table. He plopped down on the sofa. "I can, but if anyone should be upset it should be Tatayana; we have three kids together now and we were talking about making things official when I ran up in Shaqwanaya and the condom broke."

"Good to know you began using protection." Royal wrote on his pad. "Twelve children with seven women means you have several with at least one of those women. Not one of them was able to hold your attention longer than it took to create a life?"

Oscar shook his head. "Real talk?"

"The only way we'll get to some real results."

"I couldn't see what any of them wanted with me especially the good ones, outside of a quick paycheck; so I gave them the best time they ever had with a man in every way. Passion and the occasional impatience with a few groupies and here I am twelve kids later." Oscar shrugged.

"You must want this to be your last session."

Oscar's eyes zeroed in on Royal. "I'm sure it doesn't work like that. The person who referred me told me you changed his life...yeah, I'm still waiting."

"Giving me answers like that means you're not ready to confront the truth. Either we talk about how you ended up with eleven more kids after the first unplanned pregnancy or you pay someone else to listen to you make excuses." Royal placed the pen and pad on the table.

"No one with any real worth would want someone whose own parents didn't want him. Imagine how I felt the first time I experienced an erection with no one to talk to about what was going on. None of the things you talk to your Mom or Dad about were discussed with Aunt Glenda. If what she gave was her best, fine; but no matter what it was, for me it wasn't enough." Oscar watched Royal scribble on his pad.

The sound of the fountain in the corner of the room filled the silence as Royal continued to write.

"Doc?" Oscar attempted to look at the scribbles on the pad.

Royal placed the pad and pen on the end table next to his chair. "Lie back and close your eyes. We're gonna do a recall activity."

Oscar lay his lean frame back on the sofa with his eyes closed. His hands, clasped together, rested on his stomach. His loud breath quieted to a normal pace and volume.

Royal leaned against the window-staring out toward the lake. "Go back to the first time you realized the way you lived was different from your friends. When one of your friend's mothers showed affection to either your friend's dad or a new love interest. Tell me the feeling that radiates through your body no matter how weird it feels or you think it will sound."

"Weird." Oscar cleared his throat. "Ms. Ramirez always kissed her husband hello and goodbye. He would grab a handful of bottom and whisper something in Spanish that caused her to blush, giggle and give him a playful hit."

"Weird isn't a feeling, Oscar. You see them exchange affection and notice the love they share is missing from your home life. How do you feel?"

"Cheated, jealous, confused, upset and tired." Oscar's voice dipped to a lower octave.

"Tired?" Royal turned away from the window to look at his client.

"That year I realized how different my life was from the other kids, and by the time I realized my home wasn't a home, I was tired of knowing I wasn't good enough to have parents or a loving home. So yeah, tired." Oscar sighed. "You gonna tell me I treated all of those women like shit because I didn't think I deserved better?"

"I don't need to, you just did. I'm gonna ask you what needs to happen for you to realize that is a lie so we can get to the business of making your emotional limp disappear... nothing I can do for your leg though." Royal looked back out of the window.

Oscar tapped his fingertips on his knee. "People bring problems to me for me to solve. The franchise is seeing greater ticket sales and morale is higher than it has been for the team than it has been for five years. I'm baseball royalty. They consider me a living legend. I don't need parenting advice. I came to work through what is keeping me from sleeping and threatening my sobriety."

"So answer my question, Oscar. What needs to happen for you to be honest about who you are, who you pretend to be and who you're supposed to be? The man you think people believe you are would have married one of those women ten years ago. You're still making babies." Royal said.

"Two of them could've been Mrs. Tyler. Tatayana should be my wife, but I knew if I married her I'd ruin her chances of being with someone worth loving." Oscar sighed. A tear rolled down his cheek. He looked into Royal's eyes as he lowered himself back into his chair.

"Other than your parents and Aunt not knowing how to parent you, what proof do you have you're not worth loving? Is it the ridiculous success, the roster of women most men would kill to have as dates, never mind options, or being disease-free despite several years of reckless behavior?" Royal leaned away from Oscar toward a mint bowl on his side table.

"You about to offer me Jesus or something?" Oscar laughed.

Royal picked up his pen and paper. "No, I'm not here to introduce you to someone who came to save your soul. My purpose for agreeing to counsel you is to show you your soul is worth saving. Your life is worth appreciating and being the king everyone treats you like, instead of limping through the rest of your life and maiming those connected to you."

***

"That was the best session we ever had." Royal smiled. "Oscar's natural ability, charm and talent were wrapped in a grown man's suit housing a maimed unloved little boy. His immediate sphere of influence gave him nothing to build with and climb up from childhood into manhood. Each year his body developed, muscles matured and changed, but he was never shown love. His hope for somewhere to belong, for someone to claim him was deferred and no one told him he had the power to claim himself. Until he came here and the result is the comeback story of the year…from Deadbeat to Dad of the Millennium."

Gabriel cleared his throat. He scribbled so fast on his tablet the stylus squeaked.

"Slow down! I'm glad you changed your mind about him. His case is more common than you believe. Men who weren't given the right foundational deposits attempting to operate from emotional deficits and bankrupt hearts and too ashamed to admit they have something important missing…are crippled." Royal said.

MEMORIES

Royal glided down the hall with ease thinking about the first time he worked with a high profile client. Light from the sun reflected off of the platinum handrail affixed to the wall. He nodded at his assistant Ms. Barnes as he crossed the threshold of his office. "Let Gabriel know I'm ready for our session."

"Yes sir." Ms. Barnes pressed the small upraised button on her head set. "Tell Gabriel Michael is ready for him; then once you find the file, call me back."

Memories of his first session with the client Royal planned to tell Gabriel about rolled through Royal's mind. The success stories were great for lessons, but the failures gave him great insight into the needs of broken men too. Delicate egos were a chronic condition of the men people expected to rule the world.

Gabriel paused in the door then dropped his head and proceeded to the sofa. "So I'm demoted back to the couch?"

Royal laughed, "No demotion, I need to stay awake. Not sure how the clients stay awake lying there. I wanted to take a nap several times last time we met."

Gabriel chuckled. "I thought you closed your eyes to concentrate better."

The calming effect of the fountain in the corner next to the floor-to-ceiling window filled the moment of silence. Royal allowed it to transmit him back to the night he met Benjamin Jiminez. His therapy ended without them achieving the goals Jiminez expressed but Royal couldn't bring himself to consider the therapy a failure as long as Jiminez was alive and free.

***

The slim, light brown, tattoo-covered arm of Benjamin Jiminez rested on the corner of the couch as if he grew up resting on fifty thousand dollar furniture instead of fifty dollar goodwill futons. Stories about how much his mother sacrificed to keep him from the streets of his hometown that escorted his father to a revolving door in and out of jail were the stuff that inspired legendary Lifetime movies. His funny money fueled the account which allowed him to invest in social media companies and go from broke to billionaire in the time it took for his voice to change.

"What it do Dr. Michael?" Benjamin stood and attempted to pull Michael into a half-hug half-urban handshake.

"Royal or Dr. Royal, but Dr. Michael is unacceptable, Benjamin." Royal offered his hand and gave Benjamin's hand a firm grasp in a traditional handshake. "You'll find no use for the latest homeboy habits here, and my first goal is to rid you of the need to emulate the habits of people you didn't know growing up. I know your mother worked two full time jobs and did contract work to keep you in an upper middle class neighborhood where the children didn't conduct themselves like hoods. Pretend she raised you when you come to your sessions."

Benjamin straightened his spine with a bristle. He yanked his sagging skinny jeans up to his waist and plopped into the corner of the couch. "So you're on her side instead of mine. Don't forget who signs your check."

"The pillow on that sofa costs more than you've ever made in one stand up show. Stop trying to flex with me Benjamin; this isn't a competition. I'm not trying to make it or arrive anywhere. I'm here for the same reason you're here...to make sure you get the help you need." Royal focused on the soles of Benjamin's shoes as he was about to place them on the coffee table. "Take the boots off and lay down if you want to stretch out, but don't mistake my making an exception by providing your court-ordered counseling as my being a fan of yours. Your mother is the close friend of a friend. So either get serious about being here or get ready for your probation to be provoked."

Benjamin clicked his tongue. He crossed his arms.

"Tell me why you think you're here." Royal tapped the end of his pen against his pad.

"Broke jokahs hating on me. They telling the 'thorities about what they think I'm doing cause if I'm out of the way they think my money will be they money...dummies don't even realize I tell jokes for fun. My long dough come from phone apps and investing in social sites." Benjamin reached across the table to give Royal some dap as he laughed.

Royal shook his head.

Benjamin eased back into the tall pillows of the couch.

"Tell me why the judge said you need counseling before I turn your case over to someone who is impressed with you." Royal rested the pen on the arm of the chair.

Benjamin dropped his head. "To keep me from ending up in and out of jail like my-no good father." He made air quotes around "father."

"Tell me why you're here."

"Because no one taught me how to know why I'm here." Benjamin raised his head and stared into Royal's eyes.

***

Pain radiated through Royal's midsection as he fought to catch his breath. Sweat drenched him from the crown of his head to the soles of his feet. Shallow hot gasps echoed to the top of the domed ceiling constructed over his California extra large king bed. Images stained on windows of his mind. He wished peaceful melodies filled the aching voids of the memory. No one knew the intensity or frequency of his pains. Secrets funded his life and he intended to take his secrets to his grave.

"Mr. Royal, I was notified by the system your comfort level has been disturbed. Would you like the normal constitution while I adjust the room to your preference or should I prepare your room in the west wing?" Leonardo gave a slight bow of the head.

"I'm gonna freshen up and meet you for my normal constitution in the west wing." Royal rose to a seated position. He forgot to turn the system off before he laid down to sleep. Some nights he wanted to be left to process the pain. Most of his clients were unable to deal with their deep seated issues from childhood as a result of believing they would buckle under the pressure or die from the pain.

Royal swung his legs over the side of the bed. Cold marble waited for him to begin the long trek to the hallway. No children would be disturbed by his leaving the North wing. Expensive wet sheets would be replaced by chilled five thousand count Egyptian cotton where he hoped a dreamless stupor overtook him after his drink.

***

Royal closed his red rimmed eyes with a sigh as Gabriel entered the office. He yearned for the days when he couldn't remember being awakened by pain. His protégé's stare hovered over him longer than normal and Royal knew Gabriel was told about last night's episode. "We're not here to talk about me. You and I both know there isn't much to be done about it."

"Boss" Gabriel leaned forward. "We can do this another day, you should rest before your next client. Ms. Barnes can call you before your next—"

"What you have to realize about Benjamin Jiminez is that despite all of the success he experienced, he wasn't ready for it. The worst thing that can happen to some people is to achieve the success they clamor for without being prepared for it." Royal shook his head.

"You haven't talked about your hardest case in a while. Has the client ended treatment?" Gabriel said.

"Ended treatment, ha! No...we'll get to him. Let's get back to Benjamin Jiminez and how losing his grounding led him to the mess of his life unfolding all over TMZ, Twitter and the news today." Royal sighed. "As much as I despise bratty behavior, I'd take him back as a client because he needs the help. I know if he received the help he needs he would be unstoppable-in a good way."

"We don't readmit clients once treatment ends. In all the years Royal Treatment Center has been opened, it has only been done once...and that was as a favor to the POTUS when your father did it." Gabriel's eyes bucked as he opened his tablet prepared to take notes.

"Rules can be broken by the person who made them." Royal chuckled. "And his predecessor. I'd readmit Benjamin tomorrow but only as an in-patient client. He'd have to live here for six months."

"Wow." Gabriel shook his head. "We don't do that often either. You must really care about this kid."

"Not really, but I care about all of the kids his behavior influences and whether we like to admit it or not, despite his age, for his industry he is treated like a king."

***

Benjamin's arms flailed about as he paced. His breathing shallowed and labored. Tears threatened to spill from his eyes at any moment. The pressure of each moment seemed to heighten his frustration and anger. Rage rested on his shoulders when he stopped and faced Royal. "You don't even give a shit. Sitting there tapping your pen while my life falls apart. Isn't the court system paying you to fix this?!"

"The fees I receive from the court system for this is being donated to a charity for troubled young men in your name, because it doesn't even cover the cost of ten minutes for my clients. I hate repeating myself, especially for intelligent people who refuse to live based on the brilliance they have instead of the image adopted to impress or intimidate the masses. Your life is your responsibility. If you want it pulled together, you'll be the one doing it. I'm here to counsel you through how it fell apart and how you must choose to change to pull yourself together." Royal leaned forward. "We clear?"

Benjamin nodded. He uttered a profanity in spanish.

"Don't cuss in my office again. I don't counsel hoods." Royal sat back.

"I didn't know you spoke another language." Benjamin dropped down to the floor. He crossed his legs indian style. "My bad...I mean excuse me."

"Speaking four languages in addition to English has no bearing on whatever it is you need to talk about; so say it, or I can find something else to do with this time." Royal said.

"She killed our baby." Tears finally flowed from Benjamin's eyes. "We weren't sure if she was pregnant, but her period was a month late and her tits were starting to look different. Then they said she had to go do some special training in Switzerland and the next thing I know, she's gone. Next time I saw her she acted guilty and her tits were little and... I don't know, regular again. Her idiot parents forced her to have an abortion. They didn't even give me any say in what happened to my child. Retards!."

Royal nodded. He began calculating dates from when he started noticing Benjamin in the news for less than stellar behavior. His show on Nickelodeon cancelled and fan base divided over his new bad boy image created the publicity everyone said wasn't bad but no one wanted. Negative publicity for child stars signaled the demise of a career in most cases. Benjamin was no different. His popularity was in the toilet. "You know this for a fact? They forced her to get an abortion?"

"She won't talk about it. We broke up because I cussed her parents out. They manage her and were attempting to take us back to high school by chaperoning our dates...we're both in our twenties. I'm not gonna be watched like some common criminal. I could buy each of those exploiting leeches and have billions left in the bank." Benjamin paused and attempted to catch his breath but broke down sobbing.

Royal wrote on his pad. As the sobs subsided, he cleared his throat. "You used to speak from a platform of purity and Christianity. What happened?"

"You saying all of this is happening because I'm not a virgin anymore? That's crazy! I was twelve when I blew up on YouTube. No one should have expected me to stay twelve the rest of my life." Benjamin scrambled to his feet wiping his face.

"There are towels in the cabinet in the corner." Royal pointed toward a set of handles that appeared flush with the wall. He waited for Benjamin to retrieve a towel. When Benjamin turned around he motioned for him to have a seat on the couch. "I'm not suggesting anything of the sort. My question was regarding why you strayed from the tenets of your faith. Did you not profess a strong Christian upbringing and credit God with your success?"

Benjamin shrugged.

Royal stared at him.

"Yes," Benjamin sighed. "I still do; but I mean God loves me for who I am not what I do...ain't nobody on Earth perfect. They still had no right to kill my baby."

"No one has confirmed they did. You're assuming it happened. Why did you break up with Justine after what you believed happened? Her career is over and she hasn't been able to recover since your break up either. You two were better together. Even if your parents didn't approve, your careers didn't suffer. Look at you now. These women you sleep with don't fulfill you and now you're miserable while exposing yourself to all manner of disease and a child with someone you don't care about. How do you think God feels about that?" Royal's pen poised over his pad.

"Losing my child isn't punishment; that isn't how God works. I'm not David. I didn't sleep with someone else's wife. I don't want to talk about this anymore." Benjamin crossed his arms.

"Fine. Let's talk about what you said. From what I read, your Dad left your mother for a married woman and abandoned you at early age. He's resurfaced and you have started communicating again?"

Benjamin shrugged.

"Yes or no?"

Benjamin nodded.

"How did that make you feel? Your father leaving your mother and nothing bad happening to him like what happened to David?" Royal said.

"I don't care what happens to him. I'm here to pull myself together as you said. All this money you charge people and you can't tell me what's wrong with me or how to fix it? This is a waste of my time." Benjamin stood.

"So we can't talk about your Dad or Justine, but you think I should be able to tell you how to pull yourself together? If I tell you what is wrong with you, you'll never pull yourself together." Royal shrugged.

"Fine. I'm gonna ask for another counselor. All this fancy crap doesn't make you a good counselor-it makes you expensive." Benjamin stood in the same place.

"So leave." Royal pressed the button to open the door.

Benjamin looked at the door and into Royal's eyes. He dropped back onto the couch. "You just want me to fail like everyone else. Even if I don't do another show or post another YouTube video with a million hits, I'll never be poor again. That must burn you people up."

"I couldn't care less how much money you have. My purpose here is to help you as much as you want to be helped and report back to the judge. Don't wanna talk about your Dad, or Justine? Tell me why you think people don't want you to succeed when you wouldn't be successful without people." Royal wrote on his paper. "If it hasn't occurred to you the way you process things doesn't match the life you're living we have more work to do than I thought. Everyone isn't going to like you or support you. Why care about those people when they aren't the ones who helped you?"

"But that is stupid. Why hate on me?" Benjamin whined.

"You can continue to allow the anxiety of trying to understand your haters to drive you to make decisions that land you in court or let me help you pull yourself together and enjoy the fruits of your talent." Royal said.

***

Royal's right side twitched.

"You need to take something, Boss." Gabriel looked up from his tablet. "Royal?"

Royal shook his head. "Benjamin is sitting here with us and we're about to restart treatment with him. What do you do?"

Gabriel's eyes narrowed as he attempted to look away from Royal. "You realize he was just in the news for vandalizing his neighbor's car and fighting at a ComiCon event right?"

Royal dabbed the sweat from his brow. His eyes closed.."You follow his career. Tell me what he needs."

"Benjaminn Jiminez propelled into stardom without any preparation for the trajectory. His goals and dreams were achieved but no one told him how to live once he arrived. The lifestyle choices, outside of his public tantrum about losing his possible child to an alleged forced abortion, screams of someone who wasn't ready for promotion. Our parents, and if not them, someone else come along to show us how to plan, prepare and harness the raw talent that was exploited in Jiminez but never trained. He is screaming for help, so I'd teach him how to think, analyze and the difference between what he can do and who he is. The kid is brilliant but unchecked brilliance of his magnitude dwarfs into unbridled destruction for him and anyone around him."

Royal managed a weak smile. "Very good. Gabriel."

Ms. Barnes appeared at the door. She moved when Royal motioned for her to come into the room. A bottle of water and two pills materialized before Gabriel's eyes. Her eyebrows shot up.

Gabriel shook his head.

"I'm sitting right here. Stop doing that." Royal extended his hand toward Ms. Barnes. "Don't worry about me, this moment will pass but I need to make sure you understand these cases, Gabriel. I'm trusting you with my legacy. Like my father trusted me. There was an amazing man, who ruled with love and patience. Nothing crippled about him...My Dad was a king."

SECRETS REVEALED

Ms. Barnes carried a box of tissue into the office. She placed them on the table between Gabriel and Royal. "I've prepared the cart, sir."

Royal nodded. "Should be there in about an hour. Have lunch waiting on the pagoda near the East Lake."

"As you wish." Ms. Barnes laid a gentle hand on his shoulder. "Go easy on yourself, Michael. You aren't responsible for what happens when they leave. We can't save them all."

Gabriel gulped. His eyes lingered on the box of tissues in front of him. "So did something happen to the guy from your hardest case? Did he die?"

"He's still around and things are getting better. This is about a different case. If you kept up with Benjamin Jiminez, I'm sure you've heard of Dallas Adams."

A cloud dropped over Gabriel's face. He attended school with Dallas Adam's older brother. "Yes, Dallas Adam's brother Austin was two years behind me in school."

"Really?" Royal leaned forward. He wiped his hand over his face. "So you're familiar with what happened to him? His suicide?"

Gabriel shook his head up and down a few times so quick, Royal almost missed it.

"His death devastated a lot of people, including me." Royal closed his eyes. "First client I lost to suicide. One of the few I can count on one hand. But his death, his death cut me to the quick. No note, no explanation, just the memories of three years trying to help him find the courage to be honest with his family and more important comfortable and honest with himself."

"You counseled him for three years and he still committed suicide? I don't know if I'd still be practicing psychology if it were me. He seemed happy, then the news of his death came out of nowhere." Gabriel shook his head.

"He came in every few months, more like once a quarter; but before he stopped counseling, he came every month the last year." Royal said.

***

Soft grey eyes took in Royal's garden patio. Thick brown curls fell into his face. An embarrassed smiled visited his lips for a moment.

Royal motioned for him to sit across from his hammock.

"Isn't the client supposed to recline to be more at ease sharing all of his innermost thoughts with a complete stranger, Dr. Royal?" Dallas' deep smooth voice transformed into a melodic chuckle.

"I'm sure we'll have plenty of time for you to tell me everything once you know you want me as your counselor. You need to be comfortable with me enough to be totally honest. Can you do that?" Royal leaned up on one elbow with a deft and balance that told how long he'd been using his hammock.

Dallas laughed. "I'm sure you're the one I need to speak to. You came recommended by three different people I look up to and admire in the industry. They said you take frontrunners from leading the pack to so far ahead followers can't see you anymore. My music is suffering and I need help to get to the next level."

Royal relaxed. "Well, we should start with what you think we need to work on. Tell me why you were talking to three of your mentors about someone to talk with about your problems."

Dallas rolled his shoulders and rolled his head slowly around in what appeared to be an attempt to relax. "Not being able to create or write a song alone for the last five months and intermittent insomnia for the last year. I've had every physical test known to man from holistic to medical to Eastern...I want to sleep and create again."

***

"Have you ever had insomnia, Gabriel?" Royal looked out across the lake.

Gabriel shook his head. "No, I've been blessed to sleep through any and everything since I was an infant. Some things I fell asleep on and wish I'd stayed awake."

Royal chuckled. "It's a horrible thing. Tired, body racked with exhaustion to the point where the thought of moving makes you more tired, but when you close your eyes all you see is the black of your eyelids. Sleep avoids you with every toss, body rearrangement and turn to find a spot, a place, anything to be comfortable to drift off to sleep or pass out."

"Well, I won't complain about being able to fall asleep at the drop of a hat ever again." Gabriel sighed.

Royal nodded. "Complaints only produce something that appears great in our minds. They never live up to the potential we ascribe to them when released."

"Dallas was gay." Gabriel said.

A heavy silence fell over the room.

Sounds from the fountain in the corner of the room were only overpowered by the quiet return of Royal from the window to the chair. "The only person able to confirm or deny the statement you just made is lying at rest, I hope, somewhere."

"His brother told me about how he found him kissing another boy in his class during middle school. He blamed his father for leaving before Dallas was able to get a better grasp on being a man." Gabriel chuckled. "My Dad wasn't home as much as I'd liked, but I don't find you the least bit attractive."

"The question of sexuality is only able to create stress high enough to drive a person to suicide when it is an extension of questioning one's identity. The individual exploring intimacy without a clear understanding of who they are opens them up to the danger of being turned into the person they believe their significant other wants them to be." Royal shook his head. "No one can be someone else long enough to make the other person happy without forfeiting happiness and no one who knows themselves will be able to stay happy in a relationship with someone unaware of who they are."

"In less than twenty sessions you were able to glean all of that from talking to Dallas? I'll never be able to live up to your legacy, Boss." Gabriel laughed until he made the couch shake. "We might as well turn this place into a spa resort."

"You'll never live up to my legacy because I don't want you to. You're brilliant and capable in your own right, Gabriel. The standard you need to measure up to is your own."

***

Royal leaned on Dallas in the cart as they rode back to the main property from the garden. He never met with Dallas in the study. Adams seemed more at peace in tranquil, beautiful outdoor scenery. "Do I make you uncomfortable?"

Dallas cleared his throat with a nervous chuckle. "No Doct- Royal. I'm not unfamiliar with the close quarters of a trail cart. My brother and I used one for years at our childhood home with my grandparents and mother."

"Your Dad didn't believe in using the cart?" Royal steered clear of a flock of wandering geese. "No doubt he was proud his boys were getting early, albeit limited, driving experience."

Dallas grunted. A sullen look filled and emptied from his face. "I'm not sure what would have made him proud, we've only reconnected these last few years since my first song I wrote for Madonna, Mary J Blige, and Sheryl Crow went Diamond. The cross-genre hit has blessed everyone from the collaboration."

"Tough growing up in a home with almost nothing but women and being a man. You and your brother must be close." Royal continued on the path as the house began to loom over them.

"No, he was more like a father than anyone else I know, but he didn't stick around once he graduated. Career Air Force man with a family and kids. He's done our mom and dad proud. Reconciling with my Dad has been one of the most amazing things in the world." Dallas shrugged. "Not sure how being happy can cause insomnia. Do I need some pills?"

"Pills won't solve the problem, Dallas." Royal scribbled on his notepad.

"My last four songs were so crazy that the only person interested in them was an unknown singer funded by her sugar daddy. Help me clear my mind enough to create, Doc." Dallas wiped a tear from his eye. "I can't live like this, music is what makes life livable."

Royal's pen paused in mid-air. "Tell me what happens when you're not working that makes life unbearable."

Dallas banged the palms of his hands against his temples. He dropped his head and thrashed it back and forth. A wail ripped from his lips.

Deafening silence wrapped around the both of them as the sound of breathing filled the space between them.

"Homework assignment for you to give me when you return from the European leg of your tour. If you couldn't write music or sing anymore, what would you do? Without your work, who would you be?" Royal ripped off the sheet of paper with the questions written in almost illegible writing and handed it to Dallas.

Dallas' hand trembled as he looked down at the words. "Feels like the words are swimming around on the paper when I look at them. You know I wrote my first song when I was three. Momma and Grandma said I ran around singing it all summer. Then I sold my first song to Disney at age fourteen. My Dad connected my mom with friends from the industry before they divorced and she told one of them about me. This is in my blood. Words, melodies, hooks, vamps, bass lines, notes, rifts and bridges built my DNA. The instructions to how I work were drafted on a staff. You want me to answer a question that is only allowed in a world where I'd cease to exist."

"I'm not what I do, Dallas. My skills, talents, gifts and abilities are not a definition of who I am. Outside of music, inside of your heart and soul, lies a man. Before you come back for the next session, imagine your life with no clients to write songs for and no tour dates to entertain fans and tell me about, Dallas Adams, the man." Royal nodded.

Dallas nodded.

***

"Nine months of painstaking tedious onion peeling and with one session I ruined everything." Royal said.

Gabriel's head snapped around so he was facing Royal instead of the window. Royal dropped his head. "Giving someone a homework assignment doesn't make you a horrible person. Each session we grew closer and closer to the breakthrough. I could feel his mind reeling, shifting with each visit. Forcing him to face his fear seemed the only way to get his attention. I knew he couldn't imagine life without music."

"I bet Austin and his family would find comfort in knowing Dallas sought help. They couldn't't fathom his just giving up without a fight. Seeing you for three years means he tried. Does client privilege carry over into death? Even if it does, this is one of those instances where we need to make an exception." Gabriel stood. He made a lateral move in each direction and shook his head before sitting down again.

Royal's head dropped. "Gabriel, I wouldn't be too excited about what I did if I were you. Dallas wasn't ready to grapple with those questions alone. In the sessions before I gave him the homework, he wrestled with how much he could divulge. His father's absence created a vacuum for an insurmountable variety of insecurities to be sucked into the space reserved for learning how to become a man. Finding a relationship with his father in his late teens and the years before he released his first single helped him find confidence in his craft but he wasn't able to face his identity issues."

Gabriel tilted his head to the left. "His grandmother and mother were formidable forces of nature. They would have scaled Mt. Everest, skinned a goat and climbed down with it hanging between them if it would have helped them raise Austin and Dallas into the men as they said 'God created them to be'. Dallas encountered opportunities and successes mainstream journalists and bloggers called miraculous. You expect me to believe missing his Dad for a few years in the middle drove him to kill himself? Hard for me to believe that."

Royal ran his hand over his face and sighed. "Gabriel, we don't include religious reference in our work for several reasons, the most important being that if God didn't force everyone to accept Christ, we shouldn't shove it down their throats either. That said, the demons Dallas fought weren't new to his bloodline. When I met his family at the memorial service, it was clear he felt like he had no one to turn to talk about the internal turmoil wrestling with his identity issues created."

Gabriel shook his head.

"He wasn't equipped by what his maternal caregivers provided. Do I believe the prayers lifted on his behalf were pivotal in the opportunities and successes he experienced? Sure. But some kids need something that only one particular parent can offer. We both know children who were with one parent and floundering, almost unable to function, but when they moved with the other parent, they flourished. Dallas may have been one of those kinds of children, but the option to live with his father wasn't presented and he suffered for it up until the end."

"That doesn't explain why you believe you're responsible for his death." Gabriel said.

"Dallas needed me to walk with him through what happened. Tough love wasn't as effective as I believe it to be because he'd experienced it all of his life. If his mother and grandmother struck you as strong enough to climb mountains and slay wildlife to provide what Austin and Dallas needed, it is possible those strong beautiful black women didn't know how to be soft enough to love him the way he needed. Someone needed to see him for the artist and gentle soul he possessed and love him into full maturity. Instead, everyone he trusted to help him become the man he knew he should be tried to force him to learn based on our preferred technique."

Gabriel's eyes flashed with anger. "So you sent him away knowing he couldn't handle it? That is reckless!"

Royal raised his left hand. "I'd never treated anyone like Dallas. Brilliant. I mean, an absolute musical and creative genius; but so undeveloped in the areas of manhood we take for granted. He needed the guidance of his father. That man faced finding his identity and comfort with the truth about himself in a hostile and unforgiving South. The strength I recognized in him I've only seen in a few people; but he failed Dallas because as soon as he was able, he left the place that fortified that strength and assumed his sons would be better without someone like him. A Broadway playwright and male romance novelist famous for evoking emotion better than any other Southern romance writer male or female...he was a target in the South; but he blended in to the creative, accepting environment of New York."

"You think his father was gay? They had two children and he is married to a woman right now." Gabriel threw his head back in laughter.

"His father admitted he struggled with sexuality during one of the sessions we invited him to participate in the second year. He called it what we'd now call bisexual. Married to a woman who's in love with the male lover they share." Royal nodded his head and raised both eyebrows.

"That poor kid didn't have a chance." Gabriel shook his head. His breaths became short.

"Not after I sent him off with no support. He required more attention and handholding than I preferred then and even now, but I've had two more clients similar to Dallas and they are still here because I realized my technique isn't best if it doesn't fit the client's needs." Royal leaned forward. "Not every man's strength is measured in how loud and hard they can be in public or how much sex they can illicit from women. Sometimes a man's strength comes from confronting the truth about themselves and capitalizing on who they are instead of trying to deny, hide or change it."

Gabriel's breath returned to normal. "You're not responsible for what happened to Dallas. He chose to silence the voices in his head with that noose, not you. I'm sure it crossed his mind for years before he acted on it."

"No, I heard how much he relied on music to be able to live. Because of his creativity I assumed his words to be no more than the exaggerated declarations of a diva. We'd made so much progress, I didn't listen like a counselor. My instincts overrode my training and I plowed ahead according to my plans instead of pulling back and addressing his statements. Trivial, contrived, exaggerated or sarcastic, anytime a client sounds suicidal, all bets are off and I don't let up until they can assure me they know not to use permanent resolutions to resolve problems. So yes, I'm hard on myself. I'll always believe I pushed him to the edge of the chair he kicked over to hang himself. Ms. Barnes, you and no one else will ever convince me otherwise because you weren't here to help him and I wasn't able to stop him."

Gabriel sighed. He recognized the pain in Royal's eyes.

"Here is the takeaway from Dallas Adams. Before you attempt to help them with anything else, make sure the client has resolved all identity issues. Without a clear understanding of self, any and everything else we do will only prolong the inevitable. You can't live without an identity no matter how lavish the lifestyle, cisterns full of holes can't be filled."

ADDICTIONS

Ms. Barnes waved at the short, stout gentleman and his wisp thin wife. "He'll be able to see you for a few moments before his next appointment begins."

The Zenos rose together. Tatum took his wife's hand. Tatum smiled. "Thank you, Ms. Barnes. How those beautiful grandbabies?"

"Far from babies, Mr. Zeno. One is graduating high school, the other one is waiting to become a junior. They grow up so fast." Ms. Barnes smiled.

"Yes, they do. And my name is Tatum." He smiled as he watched his wife walk into Royal's office. "Melanie will tell you, some things about them leaving aren't all bad though."

Ms. Barnes blushed. "Go on with yourself, Tatum. Enjoy it all; time never waits."

Tatum nodded. The door closed behind him.

Royal pushed up from his chair to give a one arm hug to Mrs. Zeno and Tatum.

"Didn't want to take up too much of your time, but wanted to talk with you about me helping with the foundation this year in a big way. I'm poised to become the lead representative again and needed some guidance on doing this without losing my sobriety," Tatum said as he weaved his short stubby fingers between his wife's petite slender digits. "I'll walk away from all of it before I lose what's important again."

Gabriel entered the office from the back door. "I'm sorry. Must've mistaken the time; I'll come back later, Royal."

Royal waved Gabriel over to the armchair next to the sofa. "No you didn't. The Zenos are old clients who stopped by for a few moments."

"Hello." Tatum said.

"Hi." Mrs. Zeno nodded.

"Here is the donation, and I'll schedule something one-on-one with Ms. Barnes. We're here on business; so if possible; I'd prefer to fly you out to us for sessions." Tatum flashed a smile bright enough to blind a diamond as he handed Royal the check.

"Go ahead and schedule with Ms. Barnes; but Gabriel will be the one visiting you for the sessions. That is why I had him join us before you left." Royal glanced down at the check and nodded.

"Very well. I'm sure he is as capable or more so than you." Tatum turned to face Gabriel. "We'll be in touch."

Gabriel stood as the Zenos rose from the sofa.

Tatum allowed his wife to walk out in front of him. The door closed behind them and Gabriel repositioned himself on the couch. Gabriel turned to Royal with one eyebrow lifted.

"So we're lending me out to the rich and unknown?" Gabriel chuckled.

"He's known in the MLM circle. Tatum Zeno has grossed more than most rappers make in five years in six months." Royal shrugged.

"MLM, like Amway and candles. Selling soap?" Gabriel shook his head. "You're kidding he looks like a preacher."

"Funny, they call him the Pastor of MLM customer retention. No one can hold a candle to him when it comes to selling people on the dream of owning a small business." Royal said.

Gabriel settled into the cushions of the couch. "He is a big contributor to the Royal Scholarship Fund?"

Royal nodded.

"We treated him?" Gabriel said.

Royal nodded.

"For what? He seemed so normal." Gabriel rested his left ankle on his right knee.

"Pain killer addiction." Royal's eyebrows lifted.

***

"I'm sick of this Tatum!" Melanie Tatum flung an empty prescription bottle across the room. Clothes littered the floor from the oversized closet to the bed. Her husband's clammy body lay next to the king sized bed.

Tatum groaned.

"Pretending this is the perfect family isn't working anymore for me and the kids. I've packed all of our things and we're going to the townhouse while you decide what you're going to do to get yourself together." Melanie nudged his leg with her foot. "Tatum!"

His small hand flickered, but he didn't move. The stench of urine filled the air.

"I refuse to live with a junkie." Melanie rolled a Gucci suitcase from the closet.

Hours later, Tatum peeled himself from the ground. The smell of urine filled his nostrils and traveled through his body. He crawled as fast as possible to the bathroom, spewing the contents of his stomach a few feet from the toilet and all over the Italian marble floor. Parting words from his sweet Melanie replayed in his mind.

Gone with the children. His children. Taken away from him as if he were some common hood or baby daddy. No one took anything from him. Tatum Zeno and only Tatum Zeno called the shots.

Tears mingled with the bits of vomit clinging to his chin as he attempted to sit up on the floor.

His favorite gospel song rose from beneath a pile of clothes on the other side of the room. God wouldn't allow his wife to take his children away from him. They were together for better or worse. Nothing could break them apart.

"God, what have I done? Tell me what to do!" Tatum wiped the body fluids from his face with what he believed to be a clean shirt on the floor. He used the wall to help him stand from the floor. He balanced himself, then stumbled toward the sound from his phone. Missed call flashed on the screen. Dan Sloothaven, the founder of the company he'd made millions with and planned to take over one day as CEO.

"Tatum, Melanie called Fiona. What the hell is going on?! You have to get control of this before someone hears about this from the lower level representatives. Our highest grossing and best success story can't be a drug addict, not even to prescription drugs. Living in separate homes is going to be kinda obvious by your next meeting." Dan's voice assaulted Tatum's eardrums.

"Melanie is being dramatic. She and the children will be back home in a few hours. This is nothing new. You know how the ladies do things. Bigger the argument, the better the make up sex. I hope she has her IUD in because I'm not trying to have anymore children." Tatum cackled.

"You have lost it. Her tantrum can cost us millions. Rumors travel faster than our products in this company. Get it together, damn it!" Dan screamed.

"Watch your mouth. God has helped us through worse things than this. Melanie and I are rock solid. She'll be back home and this will blow over before you can sign up a new representative." Tatum pressed end on the phone. He wanted to believe the words, but they were hollow. His wife had never left the home they shared before and he wasn't ready to admit his drug problem controlled him again. The habit he'd kicked over a decade ago returned with a vengeance and strength akin to a bodybuilder who found a new strength enhancer that made steroids look like Tic-Tacs.

"God, help me." Tatum dropped down to the floor. "Send in reinforcements. This is more than I can beat alone."

The screen flashed and buzzing sounded from his phone. A name and phone number flashed across the screen from Dan. Tatum dropped his head. He hadn't needed to enter inpatient therapy to beat his habit the first time and refused to be that weak this time. Addiction could be resolved without needing someone to watch over him every waking hour of the day, like some invalid. Tatum flung the phone against the wall.

"I don't need this. God and I did it alone before and we'll do it alone this time too." Tatum mumbled.

***

Bang. Bang. Bang.

Tatum shook his head. The pounding came from outside this time. He shook his head and used the sofa to stand upright. Funk emanated from his body.

Bang. Bang. Bang.

"Yes!" Tatum yanked the door open.

A tall man holding an envelope placed the envelope in Tatum's hand and took a pic with his camera phone before Tatum could protest. "You've been served. Mr. Zeno."

Served? Tatum shook his head. Melanie threatened to leave him and take the kids back to Encino if he didn't get help with the center Dan recommended. Sixty days to check in for treatment. She lied, it hadn't been two months.

"What day is it?" Tatum looked into the tall man's eyes.

"June 1st" His eyes swept over Tatum's small frame with disgust.

His shoulders scraped the dark cherry hardwood floor of the foyer. She gave him an extra month to pull it together. His sweet Melanie was gone. Tears erupted from his eyes as he crumpled into a ball on the floor.

Buzz. Buzz. His phone vibrated on the coffee table. He crawled over, praying Melanie called to tell him the papers were a cruel joke. Dan's face populated on the screen. A text message flashed.

'Get help from The Royal Treatment Center by the end of the month or face suspension and possible expulsion from The WorkIt Corporate Representative Program.'

The number Dan sent months before flashed on the screen.

***

Gabriel took notes on his pad at a feverish pace. "You can't be serious. An MLM standout is able to afford treatment with us?"

"MLMs are the kind of entrepreneurial opportunities that have made millionaires since America was founded. Yes, Tatum Zeno, MLM phenom and now motivational speaker checked in for treatment with us six months later when his wife filed for divorce and obtained full sole custody of both children and all of the assets. When she finished with him, the only thing the judge left him was enough money to come for treatment. He still waited three months after that to come to us." Royal said.

"But they looked happy." Gabriel stared at the door as if it would open and the couple reappear.

"Tatum had to lose everything before he came to us for help for two reasons-pride and addiction. They feed each other. Refusal to get help to beat a habit he believed he conquered alone before cost him everything. Despite being a man of great faith, the MLM Pastor couldn't combat the pull of the drugs. Nothing could convince him to seek help except his daughter."

***

"Daddy!" The front door of the small apartment opened without a key.

Tatum heard a muffled familiar voice. Sounded like an older version of his daughter. "Prissy Princess?"

A scream ripped through the fog of his mind-images of pills, an alley, television ripped from the wall. He shook his head. His hand grabbed for the sheet and found naked skin.

"OMG, Dad, this is so gross!" His daughter's hasty footsteps were heard leaving the loft. Her sobs penetrated the walls.

He touched his exposed member and cringed. Embarrassment filled him from head to toe. She had promised to come visit the next weekend she was free. His baby girl could drive all by herself. Prissy Princess, Priscilla Zeno, kept her word to the deadbeat druggie Dad who'd shred the last threads of healthy fibers in the relationship he traded chasing a high he'd never achieve. "Prissy Princess. God help me please." Tatum found a pair of pants on the floor and pulled them over his naked buttocks.

The door creaked open. "How could you forget? I hate you so much!!!"

Tatum stretched his arms out to hug his daughter. His neck snapped around from the force of her hand across his face. He grabbed the spot where he knew a bruise would form later in the week.

"You disgust me! Now I know why Mom left you...ugh. I'm outta here." She turned toward the door.

"Prissy...Priscilla. Don't go yet." Tatum grabbed a shirt and pulled it over his bloated squat torso. "Before you go, I need you to drop me off somewhere."

"Only a loser would ask his daughter to drop him off to buy drugs. You could lose your access to The Works. Dan has called Mom three different times to ask her to talk some sense into you.

Gosh, what happened Dad? We weren't enough? Why!!!" Sobs racked her framed again as she swung blind toward Tatum.

Tatum accepted each hit from his daughter. Nothing felt bad enough to replace the gnawing guilt eating him from the inside out as her words bounced around his mind. He wanted and needed a fix to silence it and numb the feelings. "No, Priscilla. Not to a dealer, to the treatment center. Dan paid for me to check in for four months of treatment when this all started. He said I'd be ready when I hit rock bottom. 'Think we can say that has happened after what I just did to you."

Priscilla ran to her father and threw her arms around his neck. She squeezed him the way she used to when he returned from giving a speech on joining The Works. "Promise Dad? I'll forget everything if you really mean it."

Tatum wrapped his arms around his daughter's waist and nodded. Tears choked out the ability to form words. "I mean it, Prissy Princess."

Priscilla pulled away. "Mom says you can't do this for us. I hope you're not doing this because you want to prove something to me."

Tatum sighed. "No, when I feel like I deserve to have my baby girl slap the taste from my mouth, the time has come to stop thinking I can fix this myself. Pride goes before the fall...well I'm done being prideful. If I don't stop this addiction, it will kill me."

Priscilla threw her arms around her Dad's neck and hugged him again. "Yay! I should have found you naked years ago."

Tatum shook his head. "Can we please forget that ever happened? I'll start a therapy fund for you as soon as I get back on my feet. Lord knows I've given you a reason to need to talk to someone."

***

"Took him five years but he won his wife back." Royal smiled.

Gabriel's head popped up. "Five years."

Royal nodded. "He loves the ground that woman walks on enough to let her walk all over him. Told her he would quit the company and forfeit everything to get a regular job that didn't bring all the stress and pressure sales required if she took him back."

"So he cracked under the pressure of success?" Gabriel shook his head. Confusion covered his face.

"Addiction isn't concerned with the source of the stress. The only thing it wants is a reason for you to need to escape your reality. The drug of choice can be pain meds, sex, food, exercise, porn, work, shopping and anything else you can develop an unhealthy appetite for as a way of escaping the stress of life. Tatum Zeno underestimated the patience of addiction. Whether it takes twenty minutes or twenty years, if adaptable coping techniques and abilities aren't adopted to replace the addiction, as soon as circumstances arise it will slip back in to take over." Royal pulled up a picture of the Zenos with two adult children and three grandchildren in front of a "The Works" red carpet logo banner.

"Oh wow, that guy is about to get a reality show following his rise to riches and love for MLM entrepreneurship. That is a great thing. Most people wouldn't seek counseling before that happens." Gabriel's eyes widened. "He is doing it to keep from losing control and allowing the stress to drive him back to the drugs. Preventive measures to deal with the changes and challenges being on top again may present."

A smile spread across Royal's face. "I told you, my legacy will be done a great service when you take over the center. You know more about these things than you think."

"We will place it in the contract that our counseling services aren't to be included in this reality television show, right?" Gabriel bristled. "Referrals work best for our facility."

"The student is beginning to think like the teacher." Royal nodded.

Gabriel smiled.

GUMBO

Robin carried herself as though she'd passed eighteen years on Earth years ago instead of a few weeks ago. She prided herself on being as intelligent and ambitious as she was beautiful. Wherever her pretty face and curves didn't gain her access, a cunning mind and quick wit unlocked the door. From the time she'd first dropped her thong to garner access to the halls of popularity in high school, she learned the power of being a brainy beauty. Manipulation and enticement were the easiest tools to access in her repertoire, but she enjoyed when her intellect had to be engaged to achieve her goals.

Getting Nathan to make love to her and fall in love proved to be an unanticipated formidable goal. Fresh off her tour of eastern Europe, she bumped into him coming out of his favorite coffee shop on the upper Eastside of Philadelphia. His habits, lifestyle and preferences were embedded into her brain long before she pretended to guess his specialty coffee mix. His wedding ring flashed and shined so bright under the lights hanging over the table that for a second, Robin almost felt guilty for what she planned to do.

"You have the cutest kids. I can see why your wife, Felicity, fell in love with you-every girl wants to be with a pretty baby maker." Robin batted her eye lashes.

Nathan cleared his throat. His eyes wandered down into the crevice between her pert breasts more times than he cared to admit sitting across from the young girl. "Thanks, but they look just like my wife. She is the beauty and I'm the lucky one."

Robin giggled. She considered her plan a success as she watched drool gather in the corners of Nathan's mouth as he dropped his eyes to her cleavage every few seconds. Arousal wet her panties when she imagined how much he could teach her about sex as an older man. Her friends bragged about how much better sex with older men was compared to doing it with boys from school. "I've seen her pictures. She is pretty. Not exotic as you deserve; but regular guy pretty."

"Then I picked the right one, Robin. I'm just a regular guy." Nathan finished his drink and left a ten and a five on the table for the server. "Thanks for keeping me company. Have a great day."

Robin panicked a bit as she realized her plan wasn't going as well as she believed. A sneaky smile crossed her lips as she realized how much she'd enjoy the catch if she worked harder for it. "My pleasure, awesome regular guy."

For two weeks she made sure to bump into him coming or leaving the coffee shop until one day she knew she'd played it coy long enough. Each conversation, they shared something a little more intimate than the last time they shared a table. Soon Robin knew Nathan trusted her and waited for the opportunity to slide into the space Felicity occupied.

Week four presented the first crack in the foundation of Nathan and Felicity's marriage. Just a sliver of space was all she needed to create the rift that would open Nathan to the truth of how much he needed Robin. He approached the coffeehouse on the phone with a pensive look on his face. Each step he grew more agitated. As he looked at the phone as though plants would sprout from the screen, Robin knew she'd make her move.

Nathan pressed the end button and dropped the phone into his front pocket. He reached for the door handle when Robin reached at the exact same time.

"My bad." Robin giggled the laugh she practiced to sound like a wind chime.

"You're good, Robin. Just didn't even see you there, I'm starving." Nathan reached for the door again.

Robin pretended to be sad. Inside her heart flipped and flopped around like a gymnast on stimulants. "My mother left a fresh pot of gumbo before she and my Dad left to New Orleans to fix a company emergency."

Nathan's eyebrow raised. "Do they know you invite strangers to eat with you? That isn't't safe, Robin."

Robin laughed again. "We're not strangers. I thought we'd become friends-coffee house friends...but still you know, not strangers."

Nathan cracked a slight smile.

"C'mon, we live over in the brownstone across the street." Robin pointed toward a beautiful building across from the coffee shop.

Nathan looked toward the brownstone and toward the coffee shop. A couple of students walked past them into the coffeehouse. "Sure, my next home cooked pot of gumbo could be years away. Can't pass up one of my favorite dishes."

Robin remembered how much the Forbes magazine said he grossed the prior year from all of the movies and other investments. Most girls in her class were busy chasing rappers and musicians. She didn't require any fame for her future sponsor and as long as he could still perform, age didn't make a big difference to her either. "My mom is famous for her Cajun cuisine. Let's go."

Nathan followed her up the stairs. Dinner seemed innocent until Robin began rubbing on his knee. "This is out of line, Robin. I'm old enough to be – ."

"Able to take care of my needs. I'm not a child, Nathan. Eighteen, which is the age of consent. You're right though. I apologize, you have a wife and children. Just so attracted to you and seeing you unhappy...I wanted to do something to make you feel better." Robin dropped her eyes and looked at him through her lashes.

He cupped her chin and rubbed her cheek. "Hey, don't worry about it. Coffee house friends can forgive each other for stuff like that."

Robin smiled. "Good. Lemme get you something to drink with your food. My mother would be mortified if she knew I didn't treat a guest with everything they want. Heineken, right?"

Nathan nodded.

"Cool. Be right back." Robin bounced down so her breast jiggled then wiggled her hips the entire distance to the refrigerator.

Nathan wiped the drool from the corners of his mouth with his napkin. "This is really nice of you. Thanks."

"I have a confession to make." Robin slid back onto the stool. "This isn't my parents place."

Nathan looked around. "Huh?"

"It's my place. My school is out here and I've been on my own for the most part, except for when they come to visit the first weekend of the month, since the beginning of my senior year. So if you ever need to come over and talk, just text me." Robin wrote her number down. "My mother didn't cook the gumbo, I did."

Nathan's eyes grew large. "You lying. My wife is at least eight years older than you and she can burn a pot just boiling water."

Robin giggled. She suppressed the desire to roll her eyes. Hearing about Felicity placed a damper on her arousal when she was around Nathan. "You shouldn't talk about her cooking. We ladies are sensitive about our cooking. I mean, from what you say, she is busy doing other stuff with her career. She can't do it all."

"Same thing she said." Nathan shrugged. "I make enough for her not to work. Working to give her everything and not being appreciated is frustrating. You don't understand. We'll be fine. Not the first issue we've had to deal with. Plenty of time before you need to worry about married folks problems." Nathan patted her hand next to his on the island.

Robin flipped her hand over and caught his hand and rubbed her thumb over the top of his hand.

Nathan cleared his throat. "This gumbo is amazing. You're one helluva cook."

"Lotsa things most people don't expect me to do as well as I do. My Nonni says I'm an old soul. I take care of all of my responsibilities. Did it so well, all of my classes this semester are college classes except for one." Robin gave him her innocent smile.

His shoulders relaxed.

Robin knew that she'd have to wait until he was more than a few weeks without sex to make her move. Felicity needed to prepare for a major downgrade in her lifestyle. Nathan's drool gave her more than enough room to manipulate things to her advantage. Any man who loved his wife wouldn't accept an invitation to eat in another woman's kitchen. Time and opportunity were the only things between her and the lifestyle she deserved with a powerful rich man's arm to hang off as the trophy second wife.

"You sure you cooked this?" Nathan scooped a spoonful of gumbo into his mouth.

Robin gave her innocent smile again. She nodded. "Sure did. Next time I'll have to make some crawfish etoufee I'll freeze it until you come by so you can taste it. My mom taught me everything I know."

Nathan whipped his phone out and motioned for her to pull hers out. He pressed a few things on the screen and tapped the back of them together. "Don't freeze it, I want mine fresh. Just text me."

"K," Robin said.

***

Six months later.

"Oh God!" Nathan gripped Robin around the waist from behind and held her still. They collapsed on her bed creating a heap of sweat and body parts.

Robin traced her fingers along the curve of Nathan's bicep. "I really am glad you came by for dinner. Nothing like a good plate of food to make a bad day better."

Nathan grunted.

"You do feel better, don't you?" Robin slid her hips under Nathan's side. She wrapped her leg around his leg closest to her.

"Huh. Yes, I feel much better, thanks." Nathan patted her hip. "I'm sure I'll feel even better once I eat some of the etoufee."

***

"I'm not sure I follow how Nathan and Robin Madison are part of the genesis files." Gabriel dabbed his forehead.

"So this is another case where we have to look at the overall picture. Nathan loved his wife, Felicity, and within eight months of meeting Robin he was separated from his wife and children by being comforted by someone who crafted a plan to get next to him. He, like you, overlooked the calculated nature of their interactions because of her age. But Robin was well versed in how to snag a man, regardless of his original relationship, because it ran in her family." Royal tapped the stylus for his iPad on the arm of his chair.

"You trying to tell me this is something like what happened with Dallas Adams, it's spiritual?" Gabriel shook his head. "This isn't spiritual, it is nothing but physical. Young, tight-bodied girl seduced older man going through sexual frustration with his wife. Nothing to see here except they continued to see each other and eventually married."

Royal sighed. "You've got to learn how to look past what the men are going through and see the spiritual connotations behind it. Then find what natural counseling techniques we have at our disposal to help the client reach a point where they are ready to be done with the behavior. Most of our cases end in success because of two things: Ms. Barnes and prayer. She has been praying about our client cases with nothing more than the leading of the Holy Spirit since she began as my father's assistant. The other person praying is me. Now we don't offer spiritual counseling, but that doesn't mean that we aren't involving God in how to help the client be who God created them to be here on Earth."

"This would have been helpful information to have years ago when I began my twenty-five percent unresolved case closure reviews." Gabriel shook his head.

"Twenty-five percent is a stellar review rate. You achieved it without any of the information you have now. Imagine how awesome it'll be when you start using all of the resources at your disposal." Royal laughed. "Yes, my Dad did the same thing to me, if you're wondering. Of course, he helped me when I was a bit older than you are now. Our circumstances are different. We don't have the luxury of time."

"So what spirits am I supposed to see working in Nathan and Robin's relationship? They were two people who fell in love while one relationship was dying. That isn't that weird." Gabriel shrugged.

"I'd agree if it weren't for the unplanned pregnancy and interruption in Robin and Nathan's relationship that almost ended everything before it began for them." Royal shook his head. "Yeah, they look like the picture perfect family now, but if he hadn't become a client he'd be on wife number three with Robin, or the newest manipulator pulling his strings."

***

Nathan's face turned red. "Sandy?"

The springy curls around her heart shaped faced bounced as she nodded. "Not Mr. Hollywood himself, Nathan Madison? Fancy meeting you here."

Nathan hugged her and traveled back to the day he saw her in college. "You look just like you did back at the AUC."

Sandy waved her hand at him.

Nathan noticed the lack of a rock on her left ring finger.

"Stop lying to middle aged women you want to purchase movie tickets. I support all your projects, even the straight to Netflix movies."

He pressed his hand to his chest and pretended he could faint at any moment. "You still make my heart skip a beat. And I'd know you from behind from anywhere, watching you walk away would take any man's breath away."

"I read about your divorce on Facebook. I'm so sorry to hear you didn't have happily ever after. She seemed so perfect for you in college." Sandy offered him a sweet smile.

"Well, at least the custody case wasn't a nightmare. Once she realized we both made too much money for her to demand alimony we were able to move forward in the twins' best interest." Nathan stared at her ring finger again. "You didn't get married and make some man the luckiest bastard on Earth?"

"I did, and he made me the happiest woman alive until he died in a freak accident at his job. He's been gone right under three years. The stress from his death was too much for me and I lost the baby I was carrying." Sadness crept into Sandy's eyes.

"Sandy...wow. Don't really know what to say." Nathan shoved his hands into his pockets.

"Silence is better than something insincere. We were blessed to have each other as long as we did and our baby is in heaven with its father. No point in dwelling on what could've been. My life isn't what I thought it'd be but I'm good." Sandy shifted the clothes hanging on her arm.

"My goodness. I'm so rude, you're shopping. Look, let me get your number and maybe we can get together for dinner while you're in town. I'd love to catch up." Nathan smiled.

"You are relentless, Nathan Madison. I've never known you to be without a woman somewhere. Aren't you with some model or something?" Sandy crossed her arms over her waist.

"Don't believe everything you read online." Nathan gave her a card. "Give me a pen so I can give you my cell number."

"No, just text me on my number on my card. I'm not as famous as you...it comes straight to my Smartphone." Sandy chuckled as she handed him her pink and black business card.

"Still feisty and fine. Someone is gonna make you happy for the rest of your life." Nathan brushed a group of unruly curls from her forehead. He pulled them behind her ear as he placed a kiss on her forehead. "I'm gonna text you later and take you to dinner."

"Not necessary. I'm here on business and whoever your making smile isn't coming after me, Nathan. Good to see you." Sandy gave him a peck on the cheek.

Two months later.

"Hello, it's Sandy." Sandy's voice sounded like it was in a cave.

"Hey Sandy. Mr. Hollywood, here. I'm gonna be in Atlanta for a few days. Think you can squeeze me into your calendar?" Nathan said.

"Gosh, I didn't even think you remembered seeing me, you scoundrel. Now, look I don't want your crazy baby momma coming after me. She is all over the tabloids and blogs for going after Felicity. No, thank you, Nathan. Drama free has always been the road for me." Sandy coughed.

"Stop watching TMZ, Sandy. I'm single as the number one. Trust me. Felicity and I are co-parenting our twins well. No crazy baby momma drama, just dinner with an old friend whose been carrying a torch for you since college." Nathan made whimpering sounds. "C'mon, Sandy, do a brotha a solid."

"I hope you haven't been carrying a torch for me while you were married, Nathan. Tacky is the nicest word I can use for what you described." Sandy clicked her tongue.

"While my marriage with Felicity was great, it was great, but I'd be lying if I told you I hadn't wondered what I missed out on all these years. You were the finest cheerleader on the squad. None of the other cheerleaders had a fan club. Just you, Sandy." Nathan said.

"Text me your hotel address and I'll tell you where to meet me for dinner. Lucky for you, my last client canceled." Sandy giggled. "Might be fun."

"That is all I'm asking for Sandy, a chance." Nathan grinned. "See you tonight. Wear something red, you know how good you look in my favorite color."

"By Nathan."

***

"I don't understand. He wasn't married to Robin when he saw Sandy, right?" Gabriel scribbled something on his tablet.

"No, not yet. But Robin was seven months pregnant and begging him to elope so the child wouldn't be born out of wedlock. I won't bore you with the rest of the details because it just makes Nathan look like a victim, which he played best. Sandy discovered he lied about Robin and he ended up marrying Robin two weeks before the baby was born." Royal pulled up a picture of the Madison family.

"They are one of the most celebrated couples in Black Hollywood. He wrote a book about blending families with his ex-wife. Things didn't work out with Felicity and Sandy, so what am I missing?" Gabriel tapped on his tablet.

"Nathan started counseling during the divorce and divulged he was still in love with his wife despite starting the affair with Robin.

After several months of Robin's manipulating and conniving ways he realized he'd been duped by a very enterprising young woman. For like three months he stopped coming to therapy. When he returned he confessed turning to strip clubs and pornography to escape the mess he made of his life. Felicity still held his heart, and Robin wasn't who she portrayed herself to be in the beginning. He claimed he felt hopeless. He justified lying because Sandy gave him hope when he reunited with her. He had decided not to pursue the relationship when Robin popped up pregnant."

Gabriel's mouth dropped open.

"Sandy never found out about Robin from Nathan. He pursued her hard and was trying to get me to tell him how to get rid of Robin to pursue Sandy without Sandy finding out about Robin or the baby. Courage and responsibility were foreign concepts to him when he restarted treatment. By the time he reunited with Sandy, he didn't even realize he was mimicking what Robin did in his attempts to win Sandy. Sandy wasn't buying it and from what I remember him telling me about Sandy, she trusted her gut instincts about him having someone. Robin's antics and drama caused him to be alienated from friends and connections he had in the industry for years in the beginning of their relationship. Until he admitted he was still in love with Felicity when they divorced, he couldn't move forward with Robin. They have a good marriage now but it took six years." Royal nodded slow and paused.

"I'm supposed to recognize these traits? No one in the Bible fits this description." Gabriel closed his eyes and rubbed his temples.

"Ahab and Jezebel. Ahab funds all of Jezebel's antics and capers. She runs rampant and ruins Ahab's family name. Her manipulation and witchcraft is legendary in the church. By the end of treatment, Nathan learned how to take control and his ability to lead was restored but he allowed the situation with Robin to almost destroy his career and family." Royal shook his head.

"Well, it did destroy his first family. He and Robin seem so happy now though. I thought Jezebel had to die to be stopped." Gabriel wrote something on his pad.

"Not in all cases. Jezebel can only exist where there is an Ahab. Once Nathan took control of the relationship, Robin had two choices, leave or allow him to take the lead. She made the right choice and allowed him to be the man he pretended to be to everyone else." Royal said. He paused and looked at Gabriel.

"So when he took charge he saved his relationship with Robin and now they have a great marriage." Gabriel wrote on his tablet. "So Sandy and Felicity were attracted to him because they have Jezebel spirits?"

"Not always, some men are Ahabs and try to make the woman in their life Jezebel's but a woman who expects a man to lead will leave the relationship if the man doesn't take the lead like she expects him to do, especially if she has had a positive male figure in her life. We focus on making sure we teach our clients how to be the king in their home the same way they are in the industry they dominate. Many times these men will relinquish power and responsibility to the woman because they witnessed something similar as children or they weren't able to learn how to shoulder the responsibility of leading a home and providing for it and protecting the lives God gives them to watch over. You have to be sure that you are able to see beyond the stories the clients tell and find the spiritual stronghold and root behind what is crippling them. If not, our accuracy rate may go down and then we won't rule our industry. I know how competitive you are, Gabriel, that won't be your legacy will it?"

"No, Boss." Gabriel shook his head. "I'm not sure I can do this, Royal, Ms. Barnes has been your assistant for years and your Dad's before that, I don't know if my assistant is able to do what she does."

"Of course she will, who do you think recruited her to work for us." Royal clapped his hands together. He pushed up from his chair. "I'm hungry. We can discuss this more over dinner."

"So what happened to Sandy? She sounded like a great woman. Did Nathan end up hurting her before she discovered the truth about Robin or did she see through him?"

"According to Nathan, Sandy is married and doing well for herself. She and Nathan saw each other at the college reunion. Her twins and new husband have made her very happy." Royal nodded toward the door. "C'mon, last time we kept talking instead of eating I woke up in the middle of the night with bad dreams about cold chicken."

Gabriel shook his head. "Don't blame those bad dreams on me, Boss. You know Ms. Barnes told you to stop mixing those weird foods you like together. Chicken and oysters with syrup, I'd wake up with stomach problems not bad dreams."

Royal laughed as he led Gabriel out of the office.

HUMILIATION

Gabriel hugged Ms. Barnes from behind her desk. "You know we have to do something amazing for this event, right? I mean. He is counting on us to do something ridiculous."

Ms. Barnes plucked Gabriel's hand. She pulled him to the side of her desk and motioned for him to sit down. "I'm opposed to this entire business. But since you and Royal are intent on doing it, I'm gonna contribute whatever you need."

A smile covered Gabriel's face. "Thanks, Ms. Barnes. You're the best. Don't know what we'd do without you around here and I hope we won't have to find out anytime soon."

"Long as there is breath in my body and the good Lord says so, I'll be here doing what I do. You just make sure you get everything you need for this ceremony from him. Our plans can be changed at any moment and you need to be ready to help these men. Lives depend on the lives you and the rest of the counselors here restore." Ms. Barnes placed a reassuring hand on top of Gabriel's hand. "Don't doubt yourself, he wouldn't have chosen if you couldn't do what he is asking you to do. We'll be fine."

Sunlight streamed through the window onto a magazine cover with Lenin Everson's face under a broken halo.

"Now that is odd? He hasn't been newsworthy in years." Gabriel retrieved the magazine from the table.

A sigh escaped Ms. Barnes lips. She rested her chin in her hand while looking at the picture of the handsome man. "His story ended better than everyone assumed. Royal lost a lot of weight and sleep behind counseling that man...just between me and you. He was my least favorite client. I know we all have our demons to face and battles to fight but the things he did and the lies he told. Deception of that magnitude? God forgive me for judging but some days I made sure I wasn't here when he came because I wasn't sure I'd maintain my professionalism."

"We treated Lenin Everson? Wow! For a while he was the most hated man in America. I'm not being extreme. They talked about it on TMZ. They polled people on Huffington Post." Gabriel thumbed the cover and turned it over in his hands. "Looks like this was from the golden years when he reigned supreme. "Time Man of the Year" to total obscurity. Gosh, I'm surprised he didn't kill himself."

"We kept him under suicide watch the first two weeks he was onsite. I'm not sure how Royal forgave me for not being able to pray for Lenin the way I did the other clients. I prayed for Royal in a way I'd never prayed for anyone before that and haven't had to pray for anyone else since. But I just couldn't get past myself to pray for Lenin. God is faithful though, he sent Royal a picture of him with his children and grandchildren about six months ago. He has a modest home on the west coast and lives off the interest from his investments." Ms. Barnes shook her head. "Enough of this. I'm sure Royal is the one who left that magazine on the table. You know he is waiting. Stop stalling."

***

"Five, Lenin, five?" Ursula flung the tabloid in his face. "Nothing you say with that silver forked tongue you've used to talk your lying ass back into my life can get you to change my mind this time. How could you? Children! Those were not adults. I don't care how close to eighteen they were about to be, you stole something from them and I hope you rot in the hottest corner of hell for what you did to them. Nasty bastard!"

Lenin reached for his wife's arm. He felt like a thoroughbred winner kicked him in the crotch and stomach with full force. His plan to prepare Ursula for the lies and accusations was thwarted by a leak to a rag he didn't even know his wife knew existed. "Ursula, I'd never…"

Venom soaked daggers shot from his wife's eyes to his face. "Sell it somewhere else you PEDOPHILE! The only thing you can motivate me to do right now is commit a felony. But don't worry. You can stay in your big fancy house, keep driving your overpriced car and listening to the lies of those brainwashed drones who helped you forget the man I married. My parents have finished renovating the house in Carolina. The children are already gone and I've shipped all of my things."

Lenin dropped down to his knees. Ursula Grant made begging a privilege. A virgin when they married, he believed his stock went from private to world traded with her prayers alone. His good luck charm from day one. The thought of losing her sent his heart into a tailspin. "No one can break us apart. Divorce isn't an option. Indestructible. Remember any of those words. We wrote them and recited them to each other at our fifteen year anniversary. Don't you realize how much I love you. I wouldn't be the man I am today without you, leaving is not an option."

Ursula pulled a pack of papers from her purse and flung them in front of where her husband knelt. "If that is true, for what you did to those children and all the people who were sincere in supporting you, I'll spend the rest of my life hoping and praying for God to forgive me."

Lenin picked up the papers. PETITION FOR DIVORCE. Tears filled his eyes as he looked up to his wife's distorted face. All the love and admiration he'd grown accustomed to seeing in her eyes was replaced with a poisonous stare. "Ursula, no."

She bent down at the waist. Her face was millimeters from his. "You disgust me. If I don't ever see you again outside of divorce court it will be too soon. For all I gave up for you, to love you, this is what you did to repay me for that love and the life I worked to build with you. Cry until you die from dehydration, see if I care."

Lenin sucked in a deep breath. Lips once curved with smiles of adoration, honey dipped words of edification replaced with razors. He laid down to block his wife's path. "No...Ursula."

She stepped over her husband's body.

"Baby, please. Don't do this to us. You said we were indestructible." Lenin screamed at his wife's retreating back. "Get back here, I can't do this without you. I'll die."

Ursula stopped. She turned her head so he could see the beautiful profile of the woman he pledged to cherish, love and honor till death did they part. "I would have left a long time ago if that is all it took, don't let me stop you."

***

Royal stared at the man's sunken face and waft frame. The staff reported he hadn't eaten in four days. "Hunger strikes are only effective protests for prisoners, Lenin. You are free to leave the center at any time."

Lenin lifted his eyes to peer at Royal. "And go where?"

Rain pelted the window.

"She has everything. My children, my money, my Maybach, no matter what I said, she refused to listen to reason. Now I have nothing. Hunger is a luxury I haven't had the pleasure of experiencing since she left me." Lenin dropped his eyes and rolled the fabric at the bottom of his shirt between his fingertips.

"Money isn't as important as people. The relationships we invest in will yield better returns than putting a million dollars in the next stock that will be bigger than Coca-Cola in ten years." Royal took a sip of water. "Recognize that quote?"

Lenin shrugged.

"It's your most referenced quote. And in the top twenty most popular sayings in internet history. You said it, you wrote about it but you didn't live it. Motivating people isn't easy but you seemed to do it without a sweat. Tell me how you came to be sitting here in my office, fifteen pounds underweight." Royal leaned forward. He grabbed a stack of magazines. One by one he placed them in front of Lenin until they covered the entire coffee table. Everson's crooked smile captured the focal point of each cover. "You want me to believe for twenty five years you lied about being a man worthy of more than one hundred magazine covers, and Time Man of the Year. Motivate yourself enough to be honest with me before you starve yourself to death on my property and tell me what happened."

An eyebrow raised as Lenin lifted his head. "Is this confrontational counseling approach how you help all of your clients or do you reserve it for the people like me?"

"My personal opinion of you isn't what you think or any of your concern. My assistant, Ms. Barnes, would like to knock those perfect veneers of yours all over the marble floor. She doesn't think I notice how scarce she makes herself when it is time for your session but I don't share her opinion of you. I don't want to fight or hurt you. Despite the protests of half or most of my staff, I'd like to help you." Royal placed his right knee over his left knee.

Lenin gave him a side glance. He mumbled. "Why?"

"Excuse me."

"Why?" Lenin raised his voice. "Why do you care? Why do you want to help me? Who cares enough for me to be here? You know I can't afford this place. Why not just let me die? The world would be a better place without me in it. Sometimes it's better to give the demons you fight a chance to find a new home."

"Spare me the "woe is me" routine. Helping men is what I do. My oath as a psychiatrist is to do no harm. Despite everything that has happened you've still helped more people than you've hurt and for that alone you deserve help now more than ever. You may never be restored to the fame and adoration you enjoyed but you don't need to die. What about your children? Don't you want to bounce your grandchildren on your knee?" Royal picked up his pen and paper.

"My children don't want anything to do with me. They hate me. Especially my son. One of the kids from the lawsuits was his teammate. They tried to tell my son what I was doing and my son beat the brakes off of em. Millions later and I'm all alone. None of the people I helped remember me as more than a pedophile." Lenin sighed. "This is useless. I'll have my things packed and be gone after breakfast tomorrow. The crazy thing is I don't miss any of it. Before my company became the number one motivational machine in America, I never dreamed of doing the things I was accused of doing and it hasn't been proven I did any of it for the record." Lenin dropped his shoulders.

"Paying off five people who all described the same thing being done to them the same way makes you look guilty regardless of whether you were convicted in criminal court or not. In the court of opinion you did it and paid for them not to tell it." Royal shook his head. "Revisiting your lawsuit won't help us get to the bottom of what happened to you. I remember you before you hit your heights. We welcomed you into our home for several political fundraisers and my Dad respected you. What happened? You're an intelligent man. With all of the time you've had since your company folded and you lost everything, I know you've come to realize how you were able to become the person you tried to motivate people not to be."

"My wife warned me." Lenin laughed.

Royal gave Lenin a strange look.

"Years before the mentoring foundation became a federally funded program, she warned me against listening too much to the people in my ear about being amazing. Women were throwing themselves at me after my third New York Times bestselling book and despite my infidelities, she didn't leave me. We made a pact, Ursula and I were gonna be indestructible. Unconditional love. Titanium love." Lenin's eye lit up when he said her name. Love covered his countenance for a moment. "She saved herself for marriage, for me. And I ruined her life. Each time broke her heart, she forgave me. Most of the things people latched on to that I said were inspired by her love for me. With her beside me, motivating others was easy because she motivated me. Once I lost her, I lost any and all desire to care about anything."

"She warned you?" Royal said.

Lenin nodded. "Our staff wasn't able to handle the demands of my success when I hit a certain point and the time came for me to hire more people. She didn't like one of the men I assigned to help my ex- best friend manage my speaking engagements. He wasn't honest enough with me, she said. He fed my ego and encouraged me to indulge my vices too much. Gambling and alcoholism run rampant on my father's side of the family, which is why I encouraged people to be sober in everything they did. But my new assistant encouraged me to loosen up. More and more he convinced me I'd be more persuasive if I knew what I spoke about from a place of being able to conquer it instead of avoiding it."

Royal shook his head. He wrote something down.

"Little by little I became less and less true to what I said. Behind closed doors, I explored the things I spoke against more frequently, all under the guise of it making me more believable. Once I fired my friend all of the people in my immediate circle were more afraid of me than concerned about my integrity. Ursula stood beside me through everything. When I lost my Rolls Royce in a poker game, she turned the house upside down. But it was too late, I'd crossed the line I taught against and wrote about not doing in my first book. I'd be on the road and around people who worshipped me for weeks at a time. My every word was law, every whim and desire fulfilled before I could finish verbalizing it. The power and adoration was seductive. People think that drugs, sex, gambling and power are the most dangerous addictions but they have it all wrong. Love, adoration, being worshiped is addictive, Royal. All those people looking to me to with an expectation only I could fulfill, and in exchange for giving them what they needed, they worshiped me."

Royal's took several moments raising his head. He peered into Lenin's eyes.

"The look I'd only seen in Ursula's eyes seemed to be reflected in the eyes of every person I met on the road. My employees, the audiences at the conferences, auditoriums, graduation commencements, everywhere I looked they seemed to adore me and need me. Ursula warned me that it wasn't the same and to believe what I thought I saw would destroy me. One day I was raging about how she acted as though she didn't need me, or respect me because she disagreed with me about something trivial. I think we hadn't seen each other in like six weeks because of my speaking schedule and she wanted to go out to eat but I wanted to go somewhere she didn't. It was in that moment I stopped believing she loved me the way she should, like everyone else did. Years before the worse occurred, I was destroyed the moment I was unable to recognize the true love in her and my children's eyes. I traded the love of my family, the ones God blessed me with for the false worship from the people around me."

Royal gulped.

"Ten years." Lenin dropped his shoulders again.

"Excuse me." Royal looked perplexed.

"From the moment I stopped listening to Ursula and became consumed. Gambling wasn't as addictive as the look of adoration from the people I threw the stacks of money in front of and I craved it like addicts crave a hit." Lenin's voice dropped to one decibel above a whisper. "No one could have told me that desire would result in betraying the trust of those children. Despite what everyone thinks I couldn't control myself. None of them deserved it and each time it started innocent enough. What each of them possessed was a special spark, something that set them apart from the other seniors in the group. When they exposed me it cost me everything."

Royal swallowed the bile rising in his throat. "Did you pay off the others?"

Lenin shook his head. "Two of them committed suicide."

Heaviness hung in the air.

"So, you still want to help me, Doc? Is there some special treatment technique you have to fix me that the other psychiatric professionals haven't discovered to help people like me?" Lenin harrumphed. He dropped his head and closed his eyes.

***

"I don't know what to say?" Gabriel shook his head. "There is no proven treatment for pedophiles."

Royal cleared his throat. "Lenin Everson wasn't a pedophile. His predilection wasn't for sex with children. The reason they didn't press criminal charges is because none of those victims were under eighteen when sexual contact was made, he waited until each of them was able to consent. No, his problem is older than the ages. He started believing his own hype. Even the king needs a council to make sure the decisions he makes are sound. Not one person walking this Earth is without flaw or above reproach. Once a person begins to believe all the things his admirers say and rebuts any correction he opens himself for utter destruction. God and God alone is the only being worthy of worship and when we as men, especially powerful men forget that truth, it is the perfect setup for everything they build to be destroyed and in the wake of the fall of every kingdom are the lives lost of the common people."

"That is deep." Gabriel dropped his head back. "You think that is the case with all pedophiles? I mean he paid big money to those kids."

"Not able to answer that question because Lenin is the only client I've ever treated who admitted to inappropriate behavior with a minor and what he confessed to, while despicable to hear, didn't come from a sexual desire. No, Lenin Everson's biggest problem was becoming dependent on adoration and attention of the people who made the mistake of idolizing him. Once you reach a certain level of visibility you can't control how people perceive you and choose to relate to you. But how you respond to that attention and admiration is the difference between becoming the next Lenin Everson and realizing that true love is something only those who know your flaws up close can offer the way you need it." Royal shook his head.

TOO MANY

Lights from the camera caught the gold flecks that gave Wilson Thomas' eyes a honey color. His effervescent smile complemented the sincere enthusiasm permeating from him with every word. Each take looked better than the last one, but for some reason the director kept asking him to redo the spot.

"Come in to your neighborhood Bread N More for coffee to feed your craving for good coffee and get your creative juices flowing. The only thing standing between you and your next masterpiece is the commute to your favorite Bread N More." Wilson winked.

"That's a wrap." The director signaled for the lights and production electronics to shut down. The gaffer moved and each of the invisible people that made productions happen began the work needed to break down the set.

"Good stuff, Thomas." The director waved him over. "This one is the keeper. You made me think I could go write a bestseller and we both know I'm all about the visual...I'll leave the words to you."

Wilson laughed. "Well, I'll be back at the hotel in case you need me to redo anything."

"The consummate professional. I saw the missus in the green room. She looks like she gets better looking every time she comes." He winked. "I'd be at the hotel if that was my day one too."

Wilson fingered his collared and nodded. "Well, see u later."

The walk to the green room was quick. He opened the door and motioned for the woman to join him. They locked fingers and strolled to his hotel. Nods and waves greeted them as they made quick work of walking through the lobby to the elevator.

"This has been the nicest trip. I don't know why people keep calling me Mrs. Thomas but I could get used to this, what do you think? You ready to trade up?" She licked the spot on his neck she knew drove him crazy.

Wilson ignored her voice and imagined what he'd let her do to him once they reached his penthouse suite. Standing at shoulder height with a small torso and large derriere, everything about her resembled his wife except for the beauty mark on his wife's cheek. Small enough to look exotic but large enough to see, she was his day one. This broad, like the others, was an easy screw on the road to stardom he never imagined.

"You hear me?" Her eyes met his as she slid her hand down his pants. "If you didn't, the neighbors will once we get to the room."

Wilson slapped her ample bottom as they exited the elevator. One of the girls was upset when he forgot her name. So "sugah" and "sweetie" were the only things he called them when he couldn't keep the names and faces straight. Ever since he landed the Aspen car endorsement, women were throwing panties and everything else at him so fast he couldn't deflect them fast enough. His wife and family meant the world to him, but as a man he could only say no so many times. When they started popping up in his hotel room, he knew he wouldn't be able to fight them off for long.

Building his reputation and popularity on family themed books with a strong male figure attracted upperclass endorsements that included a morality clause. Most novelists were happy to have anyone notice them. Wilson was dumbfounded by the number of companies willing to pay him to say he loved the products they created. Six figures in contracts later and his books sales continued to climb because he had agreed to slap his face on the side of buses encouraging riders to drink coffee from Bread N More coffeehouses, inspire luxury car owners to drive the car that inspired an entire novel series about the quality of the vehicle and entice watch aficionados to own the timepiece that was turned into a time travel machine in his breakout science fiction folio.

Wilson didn't even want the fame or attention, but he refused to look a gift horse in the mouth with disdain. Most authors didn't even make enough to support themselves and forget about maintaining a family from book earnings. Between his chiseled jaw line, clean shaven by choice head and honey colored eyes piled on top of a built physique, he was what the companies called "endorsement gold." He attempted to understand what they saw because he still remembered being the thin kid in PE class. But he just kept going to the gym and keeping his teeth clean until he looked as good as they said he did on camera. One of the girls he slept with in Texas said he was finer because he didn't realize he was handsome.

"Yeah, go ahead, sugah." Wilson smiled at the woman trying to remember her name as she unzipped his pants. He couldn't ignore how much each of them looked like his wife. So many people believed it was her, he only chose to respond to the advances of women who resembled his day one. Tabloids and bloggers wouldn't pay someone on a date with his wife any attention. None of the women meant anything to him, Ericka gave him two beautiful children. She was the one he planned to grow old with when the lights dimmed and the groupies were gone, he knew she'd be there to hold him down.

***

Gabriel's eyes bucked. "We treated the sex fiend? Whoa. Jesus is real for real. I wondered who helped him save his marriage. His wife must really love him."

Royal laughed. The laughed turned into a hacking cough that racked his body from top to bottom.

Gabriel grabbed a bottle of water from the mini fridge. He passed it to Royal with the top off. When Royal dropped the bottle from his lips, Gabriel handed him the top.

"You have no idea how much a woman loves a man until you meet Ericka Thomas. Mind you, he had millions of reasons to make it work. She held his entire life together while he built an endorsement empire and would have been entitled to more than half if she divorced him. They didn't live in a community property state, they lived in the Bible belt and his infidelity would have been a great opportunity for some judge to make an example out of him." Royal took another sip of water.

"Let me guess, he watched his father cheat on his mother and that caused him to disrespect his wife and all women." Gabriel pulled the stylus from the compartment on his tablet.

Royal shook his head.

"He watched his mother cheat on his father. She was a closet freak with a sex addiction." Gabriel poised his pen to write.

Royal shook his head.

***

"I'm not sure...Shonda Rhimes offered me a deal a few weeks ago that I'd be a fool to turn away." Wilson clinked glasses with the rapper whose albums he'd listened to throughout college and now partied with whenever he visited New York or New Jersey.

"The chick who created SCANDAL? She is the truth! Yeah, that television money could be better than a movie. I don't know what you plan to do with all that adaptation money but I'd invest in some technology or a company or something. Diversification will pay bills when the readers and public relations scouts stop checkin' for you. Now I'm not saying it is gonna happen tomorrow or next week but trust we all have lulls in the biz."

Wilson nodded. He pulled a waitress carrying a tray of shot glasses into his lap. She slipped her number into his pocket. Skin tone and body type matched his wife but he knew she couldn't pass for Ericka. Not many women were blessed to have the same build, color and hair color that worked in the clubs. Bottle girls were taller and slimmer than his wife.

"Ay, isn't that shorty you had at the hotel?" The rapper pointed toward Wilson's New York piece.

Wilson nodded as he pushed the waitress from his lap. She slid off as if it happened all the time. His side piece gave the tall chick a side eye then pulled Wilson close to her by the belt loop.

"I'm ready to go. No one up in here except a bunch of washed up has beens. You promised to take me to see some important people." She slid her hand into his back pocket.

A photographer snapped his picture. Her face was covered by her hair. Even her clothes resembled something Ericka would wear. He grew tired of trying to explain how they had more pics in public than she remembered taking but Wilson knew the easy women were just a part of the price he paid to continue living the lifestyle his entire family became accustomed to living when the face he considered average turned into advertising gold. Most novelists were living contract to contract and working extra jobs just to make the ends meet. His wife worked miracles with the money he brought home.

"You got my boy right here. He's hot right now." Wilson smiled.

She shrugged. "Whatevah you say."

Wilson shook his head. He leaned down so his boy could hear him. "Time for me to let this bird free from the coop. Gotta go handle this and I'll try to slide back through when the crowd is hype."

The rapper gave him the customary fist bump followed by the handshake. He eyeballed the young girl tapping her foot waiting for Wilson to walk away from the VIP section sofa.

"Let's go, sugah." He placed his hand in the small of her back and guided her through the nonexistent crowd to the door.

She smiled up at him. "I think we have more fun when we are alone."

"Sure we do." Wilson guided her out of the door. He tried to remember her name. Didn't matter... come morning she'd wish she never knew his.

***

"Why would his wife take him back after all the women he's been with and done things to that were plastered all over the internet. The girl he dissed at the bar is the one who exposed him for cheating?" Gabriel bounced his knees up and down.

Royal watched him bounce around for as long as his nerves could stand. "You alright?"

"Not really. This man has everything: healthy upbringing, supportive family unit, great wife, beautiful children and a successful career. What would be worth having to risk giving all of that up? He must have just been stupid or greedy or both. No one with the good sense God gave them would risk what he had for an easy lay."

"Not true. Plenty of people have risked far more for far less than easy sex." Royal relocated from his chair to his desk. The wall across from the sofa opened and a television emerged. He powered the set on and pictures of the women from the Wilson Thomas case filled the screen.

"Tell me why we're looking at pictures of all his conquests." Gabriel stood and studied each girl. Several of them looked like copies of each other, but upon closer study, small things about each of them was different. "He slept with women that all looked like his wife on purpose? That is all kinds of nasty and weird but also kind of sweet in a perverted way."

Royal chuckled. "Interesting way to see it, Gabriel. Looks like he was trying to recapture or replicate something but he wasn't. His reason for being with women who resembled his wife was to deflect any suspicion he wasn't with Ericka."

"They stayed together after he slept with all of these women. Has to be well over a hundred." Gabriel scrolled up and down on the screen. "So if he had a healthy mind and good upbringing, what made him throw it all away? This isn't making sense to me, nothing about this is in the textbook. He has no neurosis, no family history...not one indicator to explain such reckless behavior."

"Lust of the eye, lust of the flesh and the pride of life are powerful draws. Imagine being able to buy whatever you want and do whatever you want with what seems to be no consequences. Many men believe themselves to be above reproach and pride will aide you in justifying actions you deem unacceptable for other people. Wilson Thomas wasn't from a bad family, didn't experience great adversity, he wasn't born with a silver spoon but he had from the beginning more than many and yet he lost it all for what you call an easy lay." Royal raised his hand when Gabriel opened his mouth to protest. "These kinds of cases can be the hardest to crack because they seem to be without a root cause. As psychiatric professionals we can dig deep into the past of someone whose been troubled or witnessed tragedy and point to one or a string of incidents and say there...that is when the seeds for this forest of trouble were planted. Not in this case. Nothing indicated the path of destruction for Wilson."

Gabriel sighed. He returned to his seat as Royal sat back in his chair.

"Each of those women presented a choice to him and each time he chose wrong. I'm not saying he didn't have a sexual addiction because based on the brain imaging and other screenings, by the time he came to us his mind did work differently but we had no proof it worked differently all along. Had he suppressed the sexual drive that led to his sleeping with over one hundred women *before* his career as a novelist catapulted him from literary fame to mainstream stardom? No, by his own admission, he assumed the women were required as part of the lifestyle."

"That is a load of bull." Gabriel shook his head.

"Maybe for you and I but something had to be done to help this man whose love for his wife and children kicked in with just enough time and grace for her to give him one more chance. Yes, he stayed with us for four months but they were four months well spent because they bought him the chance to make up for his actions the rest of his lifetime." Royal switched the screen to a picture of the Thomas family holding a new baby. "For them that chance created the love that birthed a new family and new career for him. Ericka proved to be true to the words that Wilson said, "she is his day one" and loved him enough to forgive his indiscretions without sacrificing her worth. How many women today would have walked away with half of all he believed to be his?"

"Most, and I'm surprised she didn't." Gabriel leaned forward and stared. "She looked familiar… a little like my assistant."

"That is because they are cousins. Ms. Barnes referred Wilson to me and went over my head when I didn't want to treat him because like you, I didn't see why he needed help. Second chances in my mind used to be reserved for people with no chance from the beginning." Royal powered down the TV unit. He studied Gabriel's face as the unit disappeared in the wall without a trace of its existence.

"So Wilson Thomas was the hardest to help but I don't understand why?" Gabriel dropped his head back on the sofa.

Silence drifted between the two men. Royal cleared his throat. "His case wasn't the hardest to treat, it was the hardest to accept because I didn't see a reason why he was willing to throw it all away.

We're not here to judge, Gabriel, we're here to help. Yes, we charge what some consider an exorbitant amount to do so but it is not without cause. The men we help aren't just responsible for a family, a staff or even a small block in a community. Kings come to us in times of struggle. People who hold economic upswings and downturns in the recesses of their tormented minds seek our counsel. Wilson needed our help and because God helped me push beyond judging him for not having a hard life as a child, his children and an industry was able to recover."

"I think you have more confidence in my abilities than I'm able to deliver." Gabriel sighed. He rested his hands on his forehead.

"My confidence is in your ability to tap into the redemptive powers and help of God which you haven't recognized in yourself." Royal smiled. "Study everything we've discussed over the last few months and when I return from overseas we'll discuss my hardest case."

"The one we started with?" Gabriel's head popped up.

Royal nodded.

THE ACCIDENT

A tall statuesque woman walked beside Royal. She matched his pace with her relaxed stride. Every step toward the office caused the smile on Ms. Barnes face to grow larger.

"Welcome back, Royal." Ms. Barnes pecked him on the cheek. She looked the young lady over once and nodded.

"Ms. Barnes, this is my physical therapist and medical assistant for the next few weeks." Royal leaned forward and rested his elbows on the desk. "Gabriel should be expecting me. I gave him his instructions although we ran out of time last session. He should be ready after handling my case load for a month."

"Yes. He is waiting for you." Ms. Barnes extended her hand. "What should we call you, darling?"

"Helena." She shook her long dark tresses over her shoulder without using her hands. Silky long strands snuck around her to caress the soft edges of her slender neck. "He told me you'd help me get acclimated while he spoke with Gabriel?"

Ms. Barnes nodded. "Good job, son."

"You're his mother...so formal for a mom and son." Kendra switched her attention from Royal to Ms. Barnes.

"Very good. Play nice ladies." Royal smiled as he took his time going to the sofa.

Gabriel waited for Royal in Royal's chair.

***

David reached for his son. Concern etched across his forehead as he realized his sister was more than a little tipsy. "Pissy drunk" was the term Nonni, the eldest matriarch of the family would use to describe the condition for Madge to be found in any time of day, every day of the week.

"You not the only person contributing to this family. So what, I don't have some fancy degree. My name has been mud since you brought that little slut home from college. No one cares you had some one night stand that lasted five years. Only good thing came from it is my nephew." Madge swung Michael from one hip to the other.

"Give me my son, Madge." David took a step toward his older sister. Someone forgot not to bring anything stronger than NyQuil to the party. He'd find the culprit and make them pay for this embarrassing display.

"No, I'm enjoying bonding with my nephew." Madge twirled a wobbly circle with Michael squealing and reaching for David.

Panic registered in Michael's voice.

The uncles holding David back released him and a chase ensued. "Give me my son, Madge."

A sinister giggle escaped Madge's lips as she set off toward the driveway on shaky legs. Her pace slowed then as she neared the place where the grass gave way to concrete, an attempt to transition from the grass to the stability of the pavement drove Madge off her feet. Michael and Madge hurled toward the ground.

Before his head met the hard ground, Madge shifted her weight and shielded his skull with her forearm. Time slowed as David ran to rescue his son. A cry sharp enough to pierce every eardrum within a mile radius rose from Michael. His cries diminished to a pained whimper as David rolled a bleeding and moaning Madge off his son.

David checked Michael three times to find the source of the blood. Madge's elbow had pushed through the skin of her arm when she used it to cushion Michael's head and brace herself against the ground. The family piled them all into David's brand new Cadillac and rushed the inconsolable child and his aunt to the emergency room.

Screams were heard all over the hospital that night. The loudest was when Madge's bone was reset to heal before being placed in a cast. Michael's screams were the second loudest. Damage done to Michael during the fall was unable to be repaired. Doctors promised to do as much as they could to help him live the full life he'd had access to before his aunt's drunken stumble but no one offered enough assurance to comfort David. He hoped technology would catch up to the plans buried in his heart for his son.

***

"You look well, how was treatment?" Gabriel leaned forward. "Before you answer tell me how I can get one of those "*therapists*" without going around the world for experimental treatment. I apologize, that was in poor taste. She is breathtaking."

"Ask her out on a date. I'm sure she'd love to get to know you, I've been talking you up since we met in Holland. Be sure to take her somewhere she can enjoy an authentic American burger. She is fascinated with them for some reason." Royal said. He adjusted himself on the sofa. "Cases giving you any problems?"

Gabriel shook his head. "Not as hard as I thought it would be using prayer to diagnose and treat clients. You'll be proud of my next success rate review."

Royal nodded with a smile. "Ready to diagnose my hardest case?"

The sound of Gabriel's stomach gurgling filled the room. "Sure, Boss. But you didn't leave a file, how am I supposed to do it from the story you told me about a little boy who fell under his Aunt?

What happened to the young man? Was he unable to function as he grew older? Did his Dad treat him differently? Did his aunt recover from her alcoholism?"

"The young man's father didn't treat him differently after the accident. If anything he pushed him harder to be the best. The technology that came along after the accident was able to help him recover from the majority of what was damaged during the fall but not to the father's satisfaction. Neither the boy nor his father ever spoke to the aunt again. Over the years the boy was able to make his father proud but he never felt like he measured up to his father's expectations before the fall. Some how he felt he failed his father even though he couldn't have prevented or changed anything about that day." Royal folded his hands in his lap.

"Wow, so it sounds like he received support with a bit of judgment and residual misplaced anger from the father for the aunt. You say he was able to make his father proud but didn't feel like he lived up to expectations? Did the father ever express any disappointment to the son?" Gabriel pulled his tablet and stylus from the side of the chair.

"Not direct criticism but the father was accomplished in every area of his life from elementary school to college. The son attempted to repeat the father's accomplishments but sometimes he fell short despite putting in any and all effort. Doctors performed every legal procedure possible until the boy reached the age of consent and decided to accept his flaws. His high school and college careers were without a single blemish, not one disciplinary infraction, president of every club he joined and owner of the most decorated letterman's jacket of his graduating class. A student with more spirit didn't exist within in a three-city circumference north, south, east or west. He exceeded everyone's expectations but deep down when he'd see his father look at him, he swore he saw disappointment in his eyes." Royal took a deep breath.

Gabriel stared at Royal's lips with the pen frozen in the air.

"Nothing could ease the ache of approval that young man felt in regard to his father. All of the surgeries and the damage from the accident created a deep sense of shame and he never allowed any girls to get close to him. He entertained a few ladies over the years to satisfy his carnal desires but only when the physical need was too much to bear. Instead of growing old with someone beautiful as he dreamed about, he buried himself in pleasing and seeking the unattainable approval of his father. Once his father died, he made surpassing his father's accomplishments his goal. Accolades, awards, keys to cities, stocks and bonds from people all over the world were some of the things he received but none of what he received could ease the ache he felt. Something was broken deep down inside his soul the day of the accident that no surgery could fix because the doctors didn't know it happened. Only that boy was aware of how much he lost on the pavement that day. His silence drove him to succeed in most areas of his life but the shame that cloaked him daily caused him to experience a shallow success because he enjoyed the fruits of his labor alone."

Tears sprang to Gabriel's eyes. He wiped away one that escaped down his cheek. "During the entrance interview when asked his greatest regret what did the man reply?"

"Rejecting the comfort his mother and grandmother offered for what he experienced because he believed showing any weakness would garner disapproval from his father. In his rejecting the comfort and love they offered, he had to distance himself from the women who loved him so much he never became comfortable totally relating to the opposite sex. So while his peers were dating, he studied and advanced so he could graduate from school early to enter his field early. All to make his father see he was exceptional despite the accident." Royal's eyes glazed over.

Gabriel nodded.

"He also regretted not sharing his shortcomings and failures with his clients. In his line of work he believed the people he served would only allow him to help them if they believed he possessed no weaknesses. The record he leaves will be hard to surpass but some of the clients he lost may have benefited from hearing about the losses and victories. Those two things are his greatest regrets." Royal motioned for Gabriel to grab a bottle of water for him.

Gabriel returned to the chair with two bottles of water. "You have an appointment with the crew to prepare your contribution to the ceremony in about three hours. The garden's summer blooms are full We could finish this down there if you like."

Royal shook his head. "I'll go down later, you should take Helena."

"Helena?" Gabriel said.

"My therapist." Royal smiled. He tapped his water bottle to the bottle Gabriel offered.

Gurgling sounds from the fountain filled the comforting quiet that settled between them. You could almost hear the wheels turning in each of their minds as they turned over the information shared.

"American burgers and beautiful flowers." Gabriel smiled. "I think I might like her, Boss."

Royal smiled.

"Anything else you think I need to know to diagnose the case?" Gabriel sighed.

Royal sipped from his bottle. He shook his head.

"First thing I'd have this man do is write a letter to his aunt and father forgiving them for what happened the day of the accident. His relentless pursuit of approval from his father may have been the result of unforgiveness which made him believe he wasn't loved. It is possible that his father did misplace anger to the son for the aunt but not probable based on the accomplishments and way he supported the efforts of the son. His unconfessed, unforgiveness for his aunt and father morphed into bitterness and resentment which peppered his ability to accept love from anyone including his mother and grandmother. Something about losing in his accident caused him to believe he wasn't lovable. The inability to accept love from the foundational women in his life created an emotional handicap he was unable to overcome, forcing him into a miserable adult existence which, unless he works through his unforgiveness, resentment and bitterness, may end with physical manifestation of carrying negative emotions for an extended time leading to an early death, alone." Gabriel gulped down the contents of his water bottle.

"You paint bleak picture." Royal said.

Gabriel shrugged. "No need to use a fake case study to make me see the error of my ways, Royal. I'm working on sharing my frailties with our clients. Guilt isn't something you use most times, what gives?"

A deep belly laugh erupted from Royal.

Gabriel joined him. They laughed until both men were doubled over.

"I promise you this case was not false nor was it about your hearing loss." Royal straightened up. "But since you brought it up, now that the final surgery they attempted proved ineffective, do you plan on letting people know instead of making them repeat themselves when they turn away from you? How about Helena? Will you let her know you aren't the perfect male specimen? Denying weakness is the first action to make great men vulnerable."

"I told Daphne about my hearing loss and she left me. You want me to tell a woman I don't even know is attracted to me, I'm deaf. Insanity!." Gabriel scoffed.

"Daphne left because she didn't think you trusted her." Royal reclined on his sofa. "If a client waited a year to tell a woman about something that important, what would you tell them?"

"That the woman didn't believe he trusted her to be able to handle the truth. Women hate having decisions made for them by omission of information, almost as much as they hate lying." Gabriel shook his head.

"Most women consider all of it lying. Be honest with everyone you meet about your hearing loss, you'll find liberty in being whole in your imperfection. Trust me, you don't want to wait until it's too late." Royal placed the bottle on the table. "I'm tired. Have Ms. Barnes wake me up in ninety minutes. Leave instructions for the chef to set up my dinner in the East garden and take Helena somewhere for a burger."

VIDEO SCREEN

A beautiful spray of Royal's favorite flowers covered the archway. Gabriel admired the way the gardener intertwined them in a way that looked as if they grew over the arch. Ms. Barnes gave Gabriel a quick half hug. Helena pecked him on the cheek.

Royal's picture sat in the middle of the room. Above the platinum framed photograph a large video screen hung. Each person filed into the room with a smile. Many recognized each other from television and the internet. The room read like a who's who of every major industry. Men still sought after for advice in retirement and new industry giants settled into the chairs assembled to honor the man who placed The Royal Treatment Center on the map as the only destination for those leading the leaders of the world.

Ms. Barnes stood behind the podium. "Thank you so much for joining us today to honor a man I considered another son."

Gabriel smiled as Helena took his hand in hers.

"Michael Royal braved more adversity and overcame more handicaps to offer his wisdom and skills to men than most people will encounter all the days they walk this Earth. I consider it an honor to have served as his assistant since the day he took over from his father. He is a national treasure no one knows existed and a beautiful soul retired from his purpose too soon for me to understand but have to accept." Ms. Barnes dabbed at the corner of her eyes. "Michael knew his time was coming to an end and invited several of you to come and speak today. Please share whatever you've prepared as we honor this king among men."

Ericka and Wilson Thomas approached the podium pausing to give Ms. Barnes a hug as she descended from the raised platform. Wilson took his wife's hand. For a moment he looked to the sky. A lone tear slid down his cheek as he cleared his throat. "I'm sure you all remember me and the disgrace I made of my life during my first stint in the public eye. No one knew who helped me come back to myself and win the heart of this amazing creature back after breaking it into a million pieces but I credit God for sending me to see Michael Royal."

Ericka offered a weak smile as she rubbed her husband's back.

"When any other woman would have left, even though she should have left, Royal assured her he would give her half of everything he owned if I couldn't be rehabilitated. Four months after walking into his clinic I returned home and haven't relapsed once. She stood beside me not because she was weak but because she was and is a better person than I can ever hope to be and forgave me for losing sight of everything that mattered. Michael Royal possessed a gift for looking beyond the flash and dazzle of his clients into the heart of what kept them from being able to serve others without neglecting themselves or destroying themselves or others in the process of achieving or maintaining success. Royal turned the crab barrel over and crushed it. I'll never forget him as long as I live."

Ericka wrapped her arm around her husband's waist as they walked off the platform.

A slight gasp rose from the crowd as Lenin Everson stood. He held his head steady as he climbed the step and approached the podium. "My standing here is due to the man we came here to honor. No one else wanted to speak to me or help me after the collapse of my life. If a friend hadn't paid for me to see him, I'm sure my suicide would have been the final feature story about me on the same magazine covers that lauded me as the most motivating man of the century. Watching my grandchildren grow up and the second chance to build the life I forfeited is due to the treatment of the man resting in heaven now. God only knows the demons he fought to help me conquer mine. I'll sing the praises of The Royal Treatment Center until the day I die."

Oscar Tyler waited for Lenin Everson to return to his seat. He took slow steps to stand behind the microphone. A large gargled sound caught in his throat and he waved his hand and returned to his seat. Nathan Madison looked around the room.

Nathan replaced Oscar. "My movies are what I use to speak for me in most instances but when Ms. Barnes told me that Royal wanted me to say a few words, I couldn't refuse. This man sacrificed so much to help me become the man I am today. I'll be a contributor to the Royal Foundation and anything else that promotes healthy fathers in families until the day it's time for people to stand behind a microphone and say things about me. When that day comes, I pray my wife will say I was a godly husband, my children will say I was a supportive father and my employees, as well as the community at large believes my work made a difference in the world. My priorities and life were turned right side up because one man chose to see me and help me see myself. God bless Michael Royal's soul, and comfort his family and friends in this and every hour."

Gabriel approached Oscar to see if he was ready to speak. Oscar stood to take the podium but collapsed in a heap of gruesome tears. His wife placed her arm around her husband's shoulders and shook her head.

Ms. Barnes stood and motioned for Gabriel to return to the podium.

"Royal wouldn't be Royal without making an appearance at his own memorial service." Gabriel took a deep breath. "Despite aggressive treatment including his last effort in a clinic in Holland,

Royal succumbed to the cancer that started in his pancreas a month earlier than he hoped. We spent a lot of time together in the months leading up to his death. The day he returned to work after his trip to Holland he created this video." Gabriel returned to his seat.

The lights dimmed as an image of Michael Royal filled the screen. "You are seeing this video because during my time on Earth, the time I spent with you shaped me. Something we shared caused me to be able to serve others better. God blessed me with the best people in the world to make the services we offered so exceptional that it helped only those who helped everyday people. Thank you for trusting me with your secrets. Most I've taken with me to my grave and left in the dirt while I enjoy my time in Heaven."

A butterfly flit across the frame of the screen.

"Hope they have those up there, nothing like watching a butterfly take flight. Ms. Barnes had wings as beautiful as a butterfly. She spent too much time at the office and prayed more for me and my clients than she prayed for herself. I consider her my Earth angel. Anyone could have answered the phone but I know God made special arrangements to answer her calls and each of my clients has benefited from her conversations with God. Thank you Ms. Barnes, you're gonna have more than one crown when you join me a long time from now. To the family of Dallas Adams, I've started a scholarship in his name and left a check for you to do with as you please with Ms. Barnes. My heartfelt apologies and regret will always be I wasn't able to see how to help him before he took his life. I can't say I'm sorry enough."

Sniffles and coughs filled the pregnant pause left as Michael sipped from his water bottle on the screen. "Excuse me. The rest of you have experienced greatness and some of you returned to it. I'm thankful God used me to help you become the leaders and men you are today. Let me make it clear, I didn't do this for you. God shared how to help you become the kings he created you to be, my training and education helped but your cases defied everything I learned in school. Don't give me anymore credit alone. Preface it with God and epilogue it with Jesus. If you don't have a relationship with Jesus, see Ms. Barnes after this video and she will be glad to help you get that straightened out before you leave the premises."

Ms. Barnes laugh lifted up with a few others.

"Gabriel, you are a fine counselor. Trust the guidance you get from Ms. Barnes until she retires and I'm sure if you need her even then, she'll help, but do me a favor and let her rest. She's been doing this a long time and I know her family needs her. Even if they don't, she earned a true retirement. Don't worry about when, she'll let you know." Royal laughed. "Everything you said about my hardest case was correct. I've hidden my disability for too long. Love came my way several times and I'm dying alone just like you predicted someone who allowed unforgiveness, bitterness and resentment to build and harden inside them like I did. But I refuse to carry this into my grave so today I'll tell you again not to hide your handicap."

Royal leaned over and grunted. After several moments he sat upright and motioned for the cameraman to shift the videotape to his ankles and feet. Scars piled on top of each other and keloided skin with painful looking edges filled the screen. Silence accompanied the sounds of nature coming from the video as the videographer brought Michael Royal's face back on the screen.

"Over fifty years ago my Aunt Madge fell on me and crushed my ankles which left me crippled. Every attempt possible until the age of eighteen was made to restore my ability to walk but they all failed. For years I resented and hated her but I followed my counselor's advice and wrote a letter to her and my father forgiving them for something no one wanted to happen. Each of you trusted me with the most intimate ugly parts of your souls and moments of your life. Yet, I kept my imperfections to myself. Dallas may still have been here if I weren't ashamed of something I couldn't control. No one knows, but the question will be there with me as I transition from this world to the next. Don't make the mistake I made. Be human in front of those who need to see your imperfections."

Gabriel felt tears streaming down his face. Helena took the handkerchief he gave her and wiped the tears from his cheeks.

"Nothing we experience alone is too great to be faced with the people God places in our lives to love us. Gabriel, your deafness is nothing to be ashamed of so share it with clients, please. I beg you not to repeat the mistake I made. Hiding our handicaps only leaves the next generation to learn how to live a human existence without knowing what it looks like to be great and flawed."

Oscar Tyler's distinctive sob rose above the volume of Royal's voice for a moment.

"No one who walked the Earth except for Christ was perfect. Each and every man he allowed to rule was chosen with full knowledge of his inabilities. If God deemed you capable of leading and ruling in your industry, don't question His decision. The resources and people He sends to help you are more than enough to help you achieve His purpose for your life. Don't be ashamed to let the crown shine on your imperfections. Be as honest about your defeats as you are about your victories. Let the people you lead see you for who you are for it's only when you hide your handicaps are they are able to destroy you. I'm not telling you to become a victim or expose your weaknesses to your enemies, reserve your full self for those you know God has sent to help you rule and those destined to replace you. Don't pretend to be superheroes. Give the next generation the opportunity to learn from our mistakes so they can conquer new areas and rule without crutches and canes. Let's make this the last gathering of crippled kings."

***

THE ACTUAL EVENT

Jonathan, Saul's son, had a son who was lame in his feet. He was five years old when the news about Saul and Jonathan came from Jezreel; and his nurse took him up and fled. And it happened, as she made haste to flee, that he fell and became lame. His name was Mephibosheth. (2 Samuel 4:4)

"As for Mephibosheth," said the king, "he shall eat at my table like one of the king's sons." (2 Samuel 9:11b)

CRIPPLED KINGS

###

FINAL WORD FROM THE AUTHOR

Many people, before reading the end of this book, had never heard of Mephibosheth. He was the only remaining member of King Saul's household. His very life would be threatened because of his lineage. A providential accident caused Mephibosheth to become crippled. Being dropped crushed his ankles and for the rest of his days Mephibosheth could be mocked as the cripple king.

Perhaps there is some situation in your life that's making you feel crippled at this moment. Or maybe someone -- a friend, co-worker or family member -- is holding you back or hindering your ability to move forward. You may even be surrounded by crippled kings who have fallen prey to drugs, alcohol or other addictions – and it's threatening to pull you down, too.

So many men have been dropped or fallen at some point and it caused them to become crippled. When dropped many times, it causes you to feel inadequate or unworthy of fulfilling the call and plan of God for your life. Each experience you read was about a man who needed to recover from falling or being dropped. Many times we, as men, cover up our handicap because we are told that men are not suppose to have flaws or show signs of weakness. So we raise generals that are crippled in their kingship.

The Lord does not want us to be hindered by the fall of others, or by a personal fall in our own life. Don't let others' misfortune, lifestyle changes, addictions and problems cause you to become cripple. Even if you have become crippled, you have to take the right steps to get healed because you do not have to live and lead with a limp forever. One of the wonderful themes of the scriptures is that God has chosen to turn our curses into blessings if we allow Him to. His promise to us is that all things will work together for the good of those who love Him, and are called according to His purpose. A king's handicap should not be leveraged against them but used to help their limp to become a strength.

Don't be like Dr. Royal. Don't wait till you're dead to reveal your flaw after you help everyone. Glean from Dr Royal's life.

We can see ourselves in this story. We are all cripples. We may not be physically crippled, but we may be lame in our hearts or crippled in our souls. We have no worthiness in ourselves that would require or incline God to love us. We do not deserve His kindness or His love. We are not lovely. Yet God places His love on us.

Mephibosheth and Dr. Royal were the product of another's failure, but you don't have to be anymore. Yes. You were dropped! Yes. You were crippled! But today God picks you up. Not only does He pick you up but He restores you back to your position as a king. No longer will you look down on yourself and doubt and question your position because of what you have been through. You are a king and born to rule. No longer will you allow your mistakes of yesterday hold you hostage at gunpoint with the bullet of your thoughts. No longer will you sit and pretend to be perfect and secure as others struggle to be healed. At this very moment you rise. You rise and ascend back to your kingship. You rise to new heights and deeper depths. You rise from the deep dark alleys of your past. You rise above the inadequacy and lack of resources of your life. Rise like David and slay your giant. Rise like Joshua and possess the promise. Rise like Jesus who is the King of kings. Kings rule, not just over others but over themselves. I release strength back into your confidence, power back into your stand, longevity back into your walk and peace back into your mind. Rule king rule, because today God picks you and He picks you back up. I declare that all of your privileges are restored to you as a son, father, friend, brother, and king. Live free and lead with confidence.

From Another Crippled King,
Dr. Royal
Marquis Boone

ABOUT THE AUTHOR

If passion and purpose have long served as stalwart roots for Atlanta-based pastor Marquis Boone, then the titles of spiritual leader, motivational speaker, Amazon best-selling author, entrepreneur, mentor, and spiritual advisor to a host of celebrities are certainly the outreaching branches that have sprouted from his lifelong dedication to building the kingdom of Jesus Christ. Currently serving as the Lead Pastor of the emerging Fresh Start Church in Duluth, GA, he has been lauded by fellow spiritual leaders and more for his innovative approach to ministry and leadership – a trait that already sees him setting the new standard for permeating boundaries in and beyond the faith-based arena. Armed with an endearing message of renewal, healing, and restoration, his vision has manifested into a ministerial movement of cultural transcendence.

Boone's fresh start came at the age of fourteen when he became a licensed minister in his hometown, Baltimore, MD. His dedication to education only surpassed by his marriage to ministry, he would continue to excel academically by finishing high school at age 16 and later graduating with a Bachelor of Science in Business Administration degree by age 19. This academic journey would also see him procure a Master of Arts degree in Christian Leadership and Master of Divinity degree from Luther Rice University.

The seeds planted by his early academic and ministerial pursuits would go on to bear the fruits of leadership that have seen him deemed one of America's most influential spiritual leaders of his generation. Using the power of his prophetic vision as a compass, Boone has uplifted audiences of more than a hundred thousand throughout the world through travels across North America and in Europe. Once tapped to be a guest speaker at Bishop I.V. Hilliard's "Spiritual Encounter", Boone has also shared his gift with audiences at Bishop T.D. Jakes "MegaFest". In addition, his fresh perspective on taboo topics such as faith, marriage, and divorce in the Christian community have led him to pen two critically acclaimed, his Amazon.com best-selling books "Scandal" and "Til the Last Drop."

Join Marquis Boone on his journey to revolutionize ministry and lead this generation faith first into its destiny. It continues with you.

IN HUMANITARIAN SERVICE

Pastor Boone is known for wanting to help those who struggle. Thru his nonprofit 501(c)(3) organization they help supply needed financial, medical, clothing and food to those in need in the Duluth and state of Georgia.

Connect with Marquis Boone:
Facebook: MarquisBooneMinistries
Twitter: @Boonem
Instagram: BooneM
Website: www.marquisboone.com